the Dublin Revi

number forty-six | SPRING 2012

GW00360381

EDITOR: BRENDAN BARRINGTON
PUBLISHING ASSISTANT: NORA MAHONY

The Dublin Review, number forty-six (Spring 2012).
Design by Atelier David Smith. Printed by Naas Printing Ltd.

ISBN 978-0-9569925-0-5

The Dublin Review is published quarterly. Editorial and business correspondence to The Dublin Review, P.O. Box 7948, Dublin 1, Ireland, or to enquiry@thedublinreview.com. The Dublin Review welcomes submissions, which should take the form of printed typescript only and should be submitted by post. Please supply your postal and email addresses. If you wish to have the manuscript returned in the event that your work is not accepted, please enclose an appropriately sized self-addressed stamped envelope or, if you live outside the Republic of Ireland, a self-addressed envelope with an adequate number of International Reply coupons. (Irish postal rates may be checked at www.anpost.ie.) The Dublin Review assumes no responsibility for unsolicited material.

Visit our website: www.thedublinreview.com

SUBSCRIPTIONS: €34 / UK£26 per year (Ireland & NI), €45 / UK£36 / US$60 per year (rest of world). Institutions add €15 / UK£13 / US$20. To subscribe or to order back issues, please use the secure-ordering facility at www.thedublinreview.com. Alternatively, you may send your address and a cheque or Visa/MC data to Subscriptions, The Dublin Review, P.O. Box 7948, Dublin 1, Ireland. Credit-card orders are billed at the euro price. Please indicate if credit-card billing address differs from mailing address.

TRADE SALES: The Dublin Review is distributed to the trade by Gill & Macmillan Distribution, Hume Avenue, Park West, Dublin 12.

SALES REPRESENTATION: Robert Towers, 2 The Crescent, Monkstown, Co. Dublin, tel +353 1 2806532, fax +353 1 2806020.

The Dublin Review receives financial assistance from the Arts Council.

Contents | *number forty-six* | SPRING 2012

A Cairo journal

PHILIP Ó CEALLAIGH

23 November

Late afternoon, into town with Hussein, metro carriage full of chanting flag-waving teenagers. On the wall maps, Mubarak metro station had been renamed Martyrs. Mubarak's police state had been replaced by Field Marshal Tantawi's military dictatorship. It was not the country I remembered from six years before. People were not afraid to raise their voices now. We got out at Tahrir. Vendors on the platforms were selling surgical masks against the tear gas. Everybody was buying. I did too.

At the top of the stairway, where the passage opened to the Square, someone blocked my way, demanding ID. I pushed past and kept walking. I didn't get far. One person trying to grab hold of me became, very quickly, a crowd. I couldn't tell if they were protesters, plainclothes police, or one of the mobs the police employ. I tried to keep my feet as I was tugged at. I could see Hussein several metres away, also surrounded, and then I couldn't see him, and felt hands trying to push into my pockets, where my own hands were clamped over my wallet and phone. I had no idea where they were trying to drag me, or why, or if they even knew themselves. I had triggered something – paranoia or anger, excitement or just curiosity – and the crowd was growing. I could see mobile phones aloft, filming me.

And I could see, as though in a dream, Tahrir Square, transformed. I remembered it as a sea of noisy vehicles, a convergence of major roads: in scale and chaos and noise, essential Cairo. I'd cross it each day using the network of tunnels beneath it, where the city's two metro lines intersected. Now the vehicles were gone, and the Square looked bigger than before, and the darkening sky bigger. Over the heads of the mob I saw the Mogamma –

fourteen storeys of Stalinist architecture, dominating the Square. Eighteen thousand civil servants are employed there, but all the lights were out.

I remember one face in particular. That of a short muscular man who gripped my belt, bad teeth bared in rabid determination. In another context this would have been funny. But I was in a fix. This was the bloodthirsty Arab mob we all knew from television. I was about to be ripped apart by a bad cliché.

I'd arrived that morning at 3 a.m., on an almost empty plane. I dislike arriving in big cities in the dead of night, and the one that took shape below as the plane descended, dense and shadowy, home to twenty million, was a monster. I was in awe – as I had been when I came here first – that such a thing could even function. Cities the size of Cairo and Beijing and Mumbai have never existed before. What happens when they fail?

I taxied out to Maadi and woke up my old friend, Hussein. His apartment was on the twenty-fifth floor of a tower block. Years before, when he was a student, we had shared an apartment just off Tahrir. Our old neighbourhood was now the site of running battles between protesters and riot police. Dozens had died, trying to restage the revolution that in January had overthrown Mubarak and, supposedly, ushered in democracy. It had soon become apparent that the Supreme Council of the Armed Forces (SCAF), in charge of overseeing the democratic transition, was intent on clinging to power.

We sat in near darkness, talking, as the sun came up. 'The elections are meaningless now,' said Hussein. 'The army will have a veto over any legislation or constitutional change parliament proposes. The military will nominate its own budget and there'll be no civilian oversight over how it's spent. Since January, over twelve thousand people have been convicted in military courts, tried in secrecy, thrown into jail. They still torture people. They've done everything they can to create violence, like the Maspero massacre last month.'

On 9 October, marchers protesting the burning down of a church had been attacked by the army in the centre of Cairo, and twenty-eight were killed. Video evidence and autopsies show that at least twelve of the victims were run over by armoured personnel carriers. The victims were mostly Coptic Christians, but there were many Muslims on the march as well. State-controlled TV did all it could to turn the incident into a conflict between Muslims and Christians.

'They tried to stir up religious hatred. They couldn't do it, because no one believes anything they say. The elections are meaningless now. The real struggle is on the street.'

The sun was rising. The call to prayer, electronically amplified, rose from the surrounding mosques, each cutting over the other, as I fell asleep.

I began to discern faces in the crowd, and this calmed me a little. As well as a mad dog or two, and an unsuccessful pickpocket, there were people with beards who looked like they prayed a lot, and studious intelligent faces, people of different ages – in other words, everybody was there. And I realized that there a was a tug of war going on. Among those surrounding me were people who had observed my distress and were trying to help me. But with so many people gripping me at once, they were getting in each other's way. The shouting continued.

The people of Cairo like a bit on noise, a spectacle, an argument, and even when it sounds ferocious there is a good chance that an element of theatricality, and even humour, is involved. Now that it was clear I had no bombs, and was probably not a foreign spy, I sensed a shift in mood. The crowd desired a dramatic reversal. A young man, holding my hand, translated for me.

'He's a journalist!'

Amen! said the crowd (or something like that).

'I have come here to see!' I said, tapping just below my right eye.

Aha! said the crowd.

The crowd was still swelling and I was still being filmed. Now a brother in their struggle, I seized the moment and began to shake hands with strangers. I felt the crowd ripe for a proclamation and I wish I could have delivered one worthy of the occasion. With the right words, they would have hoisted me onto their shoulders. I could have led them into battle. (To the east of the Square, a battle was at that moment taking place.)

'Get me out of this,' I said to the young man doing the translating.

The crowd budged and gradually lost interest as I regained contact with Hussein and we were escorted out by a small group. They kept apologizing.

Then Hussein and I were on our own, walking one of the streets near the US embassy, lined with armoured cars. There would be no rioting there.

'That was my fault,' I admitted. 'I misjudged that. It's an old eastern European scam – someone pretending to be a cop wants to check your documents, then your wallet ... I feel bad for pushing that kid out of the way. He was smaller than me, too ... A student probably, doing his bit for the revolution. He was taking the trouble to talk to me in English.'

Hussein recalled how, shortly after the January revolution, he had travelled to Europe, and the one thing people had wanted to discuss was the assault on a CBS journalist in the Square. 'She was attacked by a Mubarak mob. It has been a regime tactic for years, to sexually assault female protesters. This was the kind of thing people were trying to change. When the regime did it to Egyptian women it wasn't news in Europe.'

We had looped back and were approaching the Square again. Hussein bought an industrial gas mask with a carbon filter from a vendor and urged me to do the same.

'I don't intend getting that close.'

'Sometimes it just happens.'

He had also brought swimming goggles to protect his eyes. I bought a surgical mask to replace the one I'd lost when the crowd closed in. As we reached the corner of Tahrir and Mohamed Mahmoud Street the crowd surged back in our direction, panicked, and I was sure the police were behind, but then nothing happened. It was impossible to see what was going on a hundred metres away. The road from Mahmoud to the Qasr al-Nil Bridge was the only channel kept open to traffic across the Square, and a steady stream of ambulances screamed by, lights flashing – it was dark now – and motorbikes, ferrying the wounded. Volunteers held a rope as a cordon, to keep the crowds back.

The Square itself was peaceful. The clashes seemed to be focused on Mahmoud, which begins at the Square's south-eastern corner and goes in the direction of the headquarters of the Interior Ministry. Whether the police were trying to move on the Square or the protesters trying to attack the Interior Ministry, I could not tell. Even on the eastern side of the Square, where the commercial avenues of Talaat Harb and Qasr al-Nil begin, the gas was too strong. The surgical mask did no good. The gas produces an intense burning in the eyes and sinuses, dizziness and a fluttering heartbeat. We backed off into the Square, where it was not so thick.

A tent city occupied the traffic roundabout and the grassy areas in front of the Mogamma, and commerce had come to meet the crowds. There were vendors of snacks – roasted sweetcorn and sweet potatoes and toffee apples – and flags and banners and souvenir cups and ornaments celebrating the revolution. People had made the trip to support the demonstrators, to see what was going on, or just because something was happening. Probably, Cairo had never known such an open-air strolling park as Tahrir had turned out to be. There was an air of solidarity and determination throughout the Square, but shot through with adrenalin. The ambulances wailed in the background and it was unclear what was going on even quite close by, or if the police were about to break through.

Improvised field hospitals were dotted about the Square. We joined the doctors at one, set up on one of the little traffic islands, protected by a low railing. There I spoke to Dr Jabar al-Nouri, a volunteer. 'This is not the same gas as was being used in January,' he told me. A four-year-old child in an apartment on Mahmoud had died the day before from the effects of inhalation. 'In January the gas was CS. This is CR gas, a benzene derivative. We're seeing paralysis and convulsions. This didn't happen before. At first nobody realized and it was treated incorrectly. Washing the skin with water only increases absorption. It needs to be counteracted by antacids in a water solution.'

Behind us, a team of young doctors was busy preparing bottles of this liquid.

'I came here three days ago with just some basic medicines. Now we have a whole pharmacy. This is all donations. People help how they can.'

The toxins in the gas are metabolized within a month, Dr al-Nouri explained, but the long-term danger of CR gas is that it is carcinogenic.

'The US should compensate these people,' he said. 'They should have stopped supplying the military with tear gas after January.'

The volunteers showed me two kinds of tear-gas canisters. The larger was unmarked. The writing on the smaller stated that it was manufactured in Jamestown, Pennsylvania. Another doctor at the clinic, Amr Muhammad, claimed he had seen a canister marked with Hebrew script. (Such unconfirmed rumours circulate, expressive of the perception that the US and Israel are behind SCAF.)

Dr al-Nouri was active with the Muslim Brotherhood, but the party had disappointed him by disavowing the protests in the Square. Our talk was cut short as an injured man was brought in, bleeding from the nose through a surgical mask, and breathing with great difficulty.

'Our busy time is after 10 p.m.' said Dr al-Nouri, as he left us to attend to the patient. It was only seven o'clock.

24 *November*

Yesterday evening, around the time we were speaking to Dr al-Nouri, a doctor was killed just a few hundred metres away, on Mahmoud. Eyewitnesses report that the police shot tear gas directly at the field clinic where she was working, causing her to collapse and enter a coma. Witnesses claim the police forbade her colleagues from evacuating her from the scene. Her name was Rania Fouad. She was one of three people who died last night.

The tear-gas manufacturer in Jamestown, Pennsylvania, appears to be Combined Systems Incorporated. Its website describes it as 'well known in the defense industry as a customer centric engineering and manufacturing firm'. It 'follows proprietary procedures in order to promote product SAFETY and RELIABILITY – all with COMPETITIVE PRICING in mind'.

25 November

From the twenty-fifth floor, you see a city of unplastered brick and concrete, covered in pale desert dust – so bright after the dark grime of the Balkan city where I live. Even the satellite dishes looked bleached, like old pottery, unearthed. Towards the horizon, the city was wrapped in the yellow haze of pollution. It appeared ancient with dust, but all of what I was looking out at was only a few decades old.

Here, in the (relatively) wealthy neighbourhood of Maadi, the pedestrian pavements are so broken and intermittent, so frequently occupied by shops or casual traders, that you end up in the street with everything else; there is always a tooting truck threatening to mow you down from behind. The essential difference between a planned urban area and one that just happens is that, in the latter, there is no clear demarcation of space. This makes it hard for the driver, who must announce himself with his klaxon, and even harder for the pedestrian. The poorer neighbourhoods gain a little peace only because the streets are too narrow for cars. Crowding and poverty have reproduced the proportions of the medieval medina, a car-free space where a person can walk and breathe, and where the human voice can be heard.

Since I was here last, there are maybe a million more people in the city.

Those three-wheel motor rickshaws I associate with south Asia have appeared. There were none six years ago.

Cairo's population density is nearly the same as that of New York, at just over 27,000 persons per square kilometre, but Cairo has only two metro lines, which intersect at Tahrir. There are no bus lanes, no light rail system, and virtually no usable footpaths outside the central commercial area. There is a permanent traffic jam, and the air is poisoned. During Mubarak's long rule the organizational power of government withdrew from the task of providing public transport. The collapse of other public services mirrors the trend in transportation.

This lazy talk about 'the developing world' – newspaper shorthand or neoliberal guff – seems constructed to disregard the places that have been stagnating or decaying for decades, or where a certain technological and economic progress takes place without doing anyone much good. The poor cities of the world are homogenizing, becoming each other; the deterioration of every public space into disorder and dirt and noise makes them all the same.

Cairo is a broken machine. The state does not intend to fix it.

26 November

I'm supposed to be an election observer. It's not happening. SCAF has not permitted official foreign monitors, so the only observers are with NGOs, operating unofficially. SCAF is stirring up allegations of foreign involvement in the civil unrest and there have been some reports of attacks against foreigners. I can't verify these reports. It may be that the NGOs operating here are trying now to discourage foreign participation in their work because of the allegations about meddling. In any case, I can get no response from the organization that is supposed to be training me tomorrow.

27 November

Spent the evening speaking with Shahir, an information studies student who publishes his own college newspaper, writing it with his friends, laying it out on his computer at home. Studious type, well off family, nothing radical about him. He spent the last couple of days in Tahrir. 'The more of us there are, the harder it is to beat us all.'

Shahir and his friends get their information from satellite channels such as Al Jazeera, and regularly updated news blogs on YouTube. The regime uses state television as its mouthpiece, and the 'independent' stations, owned by financial interests connected to the regime, fall into line. At this point the military and the oligarchs are a single caste, and are seeking to avoid being called to account, like Mubarak, for the way their riches were acquired and the brutality by which they are defended.

Joseph Brodsky wrote that the aged dictator 'clings to power as any elderly person does to his pension or savings'. Mubarak has been jettisoned, but Tantawi and the generals still speak their old language, and to the young it is lies and nonsense. This is a revolution of the young against the old. A revolution of common sense against meaninglessness. The generals defend themselves using conscripts from the countryside. Shahir tells an anecdote about an officer selecting men to attack protesters. (Anecdote? I think he said he saw it on YouTube ...) The officer tells those who can read to step to the left, then those who are illiterate to step to the right. Those left standing in the middle get the mission.

28 November

Election day. I visited a couple of polling stations with Hussein and Shahir. We had to take the metro to get to Shahir's, and the whole thing took a couple of hours. (Where you vote depends on the serial number on your ID card.) There was the same mix of order and chaos you see everywhere, and how much of the procedural confusion is tactical is hard to say. Anything that frustrates the will of the people is in the interest of SCAF.

The old had their revolution in the fifties, back when Tantawi and

Mubarak were lads, and they must find it staggering that the young are in such a rush to unleash disorder, to pull apart their stable edifice of interests and treaties. Nasser, with his pan-Arabism and anti-colonial stance, was Guevara and Castro rolled into one. Just as the colonial power of Britain and France was ebbing, he asserted the Egyptian nation and the Arab cause, wrested back the Suez Canal, assisted liberation struggles in Algeria and Yemen, hosted the Arab League at Tahrir (Liberation) Square.

The parliamentary system that preceded Nasser's coup had dithered over land reform for decades. Nasser swept the feudal interests aside, enforcing a hundred-acre ceiling on the size of a single family's holding, redistributing land from landlords to the peasantry, established free education and health for the masses. The area of cultivated land grew by a third. The accompanying improvements and modernization of industry and infrastructure allowed the economy to grow at an annual rate of 9 per cent for a decade. Unemployment and inflation were at record lows throughout the sixties and seventies. Egypt was on a track comparable to those of South Korea and Chile. In creating a state and military bureaucracy, Nasser created an entire social class. Heavy industry was established, as were massive infrastructural and engineering projects, the greatest of which was the Aswan dam (built by the Soviets).

But Nasser's revolution was based to an unhealthy degree on personal authority. It quickly ran up against the wall of Israeli military superiority. Nasser created a police and military state that made it easy for his successors, Sadat and Mubarak, to switch from socialism and Arab nationalism to alliance with the US–Israeli project. The army went from protecting the borders to protecting the generals who were now also the directors of secretive state monopolies and traders in real estate. By 2005, when I was living in Cairo, the trade minister was a major shareholder in one of the country's largest consumer goods empires, the minister for health was an entrepreneur in the healthcare industry and the Minister for Agriculture was the country's biggest wheat trader. Cronyism backed by guns.

29 November

The news coming in is that the Muslim Brotherhood's Freedom and Justice Party will be the largest party in the toothless parliament, followed by the fundamentalist Salafis.

Coming up from Sadat metro today, into Tahrir, there was the smell of piss, then the drifting smoke from the vendors of sweetcorn and sweet potatoes. The vendors were as numerous as the protesters, the tent city now bedraggled and sad, looking more like the aftermath of a natural disaster than the overthrow of a regime.

Yet this was still the place to protest, if the protesters could hold on. Tahrir Square really is the centre of the Arab world. It is at the heart of the biggest city in Africa or the Middle East. The headquarters of the Arab League is there on the south-west corner, towards Qasr al-Nil bridge. Important ministries are dotted about the vicinity, the financial and commercial district backs onto it, and the Museum of Egyptian Antiquities is on the north side. Most imposing of all, the Mogamma, on the south side, still with the lights out, a gift from the Soviet Union, completed in 1953, just in time for Nasser's revolution in 1954. In those days, the Soviet Union was the model for the transformation of a backward agrarian nation into a world power.

North of the Square past the Museum is the burned-out shell of the thirteen-storey headquarters of Mubarak's (now dissolved) National Democratic Party. It went up in smoke on 28 January, three days after the anti-government protests began, and what a sight that must have been, after nearly six decades of one-party rule. Now there is litter everywhere and graffiti on the walls and the statues and monuments. Once the Square made statements about the power of the regime, about Egyptian culture, about Egypt's economic power and its role in the world. Now it is a space where anyone can come and daub a slogan or pick up a loudhailer. Crowds march back and forth as if they are going somewhere, speeches are made, the crowds disperse, and new crowds form.

The military, for now, are letting the protesters hold the Square, and perhaps it is for that very reason, or because the vote has gone smoothly, that the crowds have thinned out. Perhaps people feel they have won. I visited the doctors I had spoken to on the night when the tear gas was drifting through. Their heroic little encampment is quiet now that the fighting has stopped. A poor man in a djellaba was having a scrape on his arm disinfected. Dr Amr, the younger doctor, only recently qualified, was sad and discouraged at the way the protest was petering out. For him, this is defeat; the military are still in charge. He works in a state hospital, probably earns nothing. I noticed again that his teeth are very bad. Can a doctor not afford a dentist?

30 November

Binyamin Netanyahu, Israeli Prime Minister, is expressing his concern that Egypt will not respect its international treaties, now that the guarantor of stability, a military dictatorship, is showing cracks.

I suppose I was about twelve when I first read about the Holocaust. The events were not yet forty years old. You could hardly call it history. But it already seemed to me part of a distant past, from a time when people did terrible things that they would never do now. Thirty years on, the Holocaust has become, for me, an immediate fact. It happened yesterday, and what astounds me is the world's forgetfulness, how it carries on as though nothing has happened. Surely all projects should be put on hold for a few centuries of quiet reflection on that disaster.

I'm reading Saul Bellow's *Mr Sammler's Planet*, a rich poem to chaos and disorder. The protagonist is an elderly Holocaust survivor, now living in the New York of the late 1960s. 'Like many people who had seen the world collapse once, Mr Sammler entertained the possibility it might collapse twice.'

So we can't blame Sammler if his antennae for disorder are on the sensitive side:

The many impressions and experiences of life seemed no longer to occur each in its own proper space, in sequence, each with its recognizable religious or aesthetic importance, but human beings suffered the humiliations of inconsequence, of confused styles, of a long life containing several separate lives ... Compelling the frail person to receive, to register, depriving him ... of the power to impart design.

This is the countercultural revolution of the spoiled kids of the sixties, allowing the reader to interpret what Sammler is witnessing not as tragedy, but the ongoing comedy of civilization.

They're yelling from the loudspeakers now; at times the muffled calls from all the minarets coalesce into something like a Latin chant, resonant under a cathedral vault.

Now, if you have seen politics debased, and the disorder of the world confirmed by the dirt in the street, the collapse of all institutions of social protection, the breakdown in the connection between the words of the rulers and the facts on the ground, would you not be tempted to return to certain basics, including that of 'God is the only reality' (translated less effectively, I believe, as 'There is no God but God'), and to rebuild from there?

The success of the Muslim Brotherhood's Freedom and Justice Party in the elections is due to decades of their work in the neighbourhoods. The Brotherhood has created a matrix of social services in health and education and even transport, gives food to the poor, provides assistance to job-seekers and accommodation to out-of-town students. In other words, it does what the state used to do. While the state lingers only as brute authority, society at the level of the family, the neighbourhood and the mosque has remained the repository of values. Islam, in this context, is shorthand for basic decency in dealings between people.

Joseph Brodsky (again), on the Roman Empire under Diocletian and Constantine:

The philanthropy of the Christian Church at this time was, if not an alternative to the state economy, then at least a recourse for a considerable part of the population, the have-nots. To a large extent, the popularity of Christianity was based not so much on the equality of souls before the Lord as on the tangible – for the have-nots – fruits of an organized system of mutual assistance. It was in its way a combination of food stamps and the Red Cross. Neither Neoplatonism nor the cult of Isis organized anything of the kind. In this, frankly, lay their mistake.

The Christians pulled off a revolution in the crumbling free-trade area that was the Roman Empire because they practised something of what they preached. The more debased a polity becomes, the greater the attraction of a movement that says people should be nice to each other.

1 December

Near Tahrir I had a meeting with a contact who used to work for the US embassy and is now a political activist. He told me of attending a meeting several months previously between an Egyptian Air Force general and top members of the US Senate Armed Services Committee. American support for SCAF, and the $1.3 billion in military aid the old regime became accustomed to, is rock solid. Changing US policy towards Egypt, it seems, requires too much imagination. The bottom line for the US is Egypt's relations with Israel, and with Hamas-ruled Gaza. Egypt is co-enforcer of the Israeli blockade of Gaza; in effect it has ceded control of the Egypt–Gaza border to Israel. Hamas representatives told my source that they expect no change from Egypt for the next decade.

2 December

In the evening, I met up with my old friend Ayman. He suggested meeting in a place called Horeia, where they serve beer (prohibition prevails in Hussein's apartment). From the street, through the open doors, Horeia looked like a teahouse; the beer-drinking section was discreetly out of view. Ayman looks the same as when we used to head out of the city on trips, him driving, the rest of us passing around a bottle of arak. He's still a bit plump about the middle and has a youthful expression in his face, the eyes either mischievous or shifty, depending how you look at him. He's left his job in a government institute and expanded his import-export business, and now employs eighteen people.

He was in the Square back in January; then the stories started in the media about people being attacked by armed robbers. This is what happens in a police state when the police melt away. Gunfire could be heard everywhere, the jails had emptied (or been emptied by the authorities), police stations had been looted of weaponry, and public television was fanning hysteria by depicting a political revolution as a civil breakdown, an explosion of the criminality that lurks beneath every civilized society. In the end, things weren't so bad. Society functioned quite well without the state. Ayman stayed home to protect his family, and got to know everybody in his block for the first time.

I asked Ayman whom he had voted for.

'Muslim Brotherhood. They're organized and have some political experience. I don't know if they will be better, but they won't be worse.'

Ayman recalls his youth as a time when life was more leisurely, safer. He sees the disintegration of services and of values, in a city which just grows bigger and harsher and more stressful. Ayman comes from a modest background but was able to get an education up to third level entirely free. 'Now the state system would prepare you for a life of crime.' Ayman described trying to renew his driving licence and getting it done in half an hour with a fifty giné (eight euro) bribe. He can afford it. Those who can't spend two days being given the runaround.

In the press today: customs officials in Suez reveal that the Interior Ministry is in the process of receiving twenty-one tons of tear gas from the US. The supplier is that manufacturer in Pennsylvania – Combined Systems Inc. I don't think the US government supplies Egypt with tear gas directly, in the way Dr al-Nouri suggested. But I imagine the annual $1.3 billion in military funding comes with a strong suggestion that it be spent on contracts with US companies.

3 December

Visited at his home the activist, writer and politician Ahmed Naguib, who was an unsuccessful candidate in last week's election for a party founded largely by dissidents from the Muslim Brotherhood. He describes the Brotherhood as an organization that in many ways mirrors the state – its leaders are in their seventies and have authoritarian tendencies. He believes the Tahrir violence was engineered by the SCAF to distract from the elections, and to pull the Brotherhood into conflict so the military could cancel the vote. The Brothers didn't fall for it; they are waiting for their toothless parliament, from there to make a stand or make a deal. Ahmed had an ugly wound on his shin from a rock thrown by a soldier. He's on antibiotics for it because he's diabetic and such things don't heal well.

As the regime plays for time, it is hard know how much design lies behind the most confusing elections a mind could invent. A parliament with no power but the power to talk is being elected in three stages, by region, over several months. Ahmed had found bundles of ballot papers blowing around a football field near a polling station. He showed me one of the papers, on which he was listed under a form of his name that made it hard to locate on a sprawling list of some 130 candidates. The candidates were each designated as 'worker', 'farmer' or 'non-worker' – a Nasserite provision, still in place, that requires that half of those elected be either workers or farmers.

Ahmed described setting out on 25 January, one of five people marching from a mosque in the suburb of Nasr City, the crowd growing along the twenty-kilometre walk to the centre, the lines of soldiers falling back and running before the protesters, people climbing up the face of a three-storey building to pull down posters of Mubarak, the soldiers abandoning their defence of Tahrir, the crowd chanting with one breath: 'We are men!' The euphoria at the collapse of the symbols of oppressive authority. In the following days Ahmed stayed with the protesters around the Square, working out of a travel agency, developing a media bureau to get information out to reporters. Sleepless, adrenalin-charged days of revolution and solidarity.

'And now,' says Ahmed, 'politically, with SCAF, we're back at square one.'

4 December

Went into town today to see Sherif, a new contact. He lives in an old building on Qasr al-Nil street, just off Tahrir. He answered the door, six in the evening, wearing his pyjamas. His place was disordered and musty, a real bachelor pad. Stacks of books leaned against the wall, in English and Arabic, along with crates of medical supplies. His place had been busy during the disturbances, people coming and going. Standard wisdom on tear gas is that it sinks, but the gas came up even here, to the seventh floor. He offered me tea or something to smoke. I took the tea and we went out onto the balcony, with its view over the streets and the roofs of the lower buildings. He told me the best rioters were the ultras, the football supporters. That was interesting; in healthy democracies football supporters have to riot just for the sake of it, but in a country like Egypt they can put their their rock-throwing to political use, and the advantages of an organized firm are apparent. The soldiers shoot gas and bullets (not always rubber) and the ultras insult them by throwing firecrackers back.

I looked down at the centre of Cairo, a European city in conception and architecture. Medieval Cairo was always a little inland from the banks of the Nile, which were marshy and prone to flooding. Ali Pasha, the great nineteenth-century modernizer, set out the modern city along the river banks. The same streets now have a beaten, dirty look. I liked Qasr al-Nil emptied of traffic, diverted due to the ongoing protests at Tahrir.

The old photographs show a carless city, the architectural conception without the clutter, so that the familiar places always look like an impossibly quiet bright Sunday morning, after everything has been swept. The bourgeois idea of civilized city living. The centre is a shadow of its former self. Even the cafés look like worn-out versions of something that existed sixty years ago. The rich have retreated from the chaos and noise to enclaves and planned communities, to enjoy space and greenery behind high walls. Gone too, as a result of Nasser's nationalism, is the cosmopolitan element that was always a part of the fabric of Cairo – the Armenian and Greek and other long-established communities. Cairo's ancient Jewish population – once numbering 75,000 – is now history, a victim of both Arab and Israeli national projects.

Sadat's solution to the lack of a national vision after the death of Nasser, and the cultural impoverishment caused by the lack of diversity, was the embracing of social conservatism. The rise of political Islam has come about by default, the result of a process of discarding ideas.

5 *December*

Spent the evening walking about with Ayman. He'd come from voting in the runoff round, up in Nasr City.

'The Brotherhood again?' I asked.

'Yes.'

'Thanks. You people want to take away my beer.'

'No! Just for honesty, and no stealing.'

We strolled in the Talaat Harb area, where I had been choking on tear gas not two weeks ago. It looked normal again. It was a nostalgic walk for me, because this is the area that was my home when I came to Cairo six years ago, these were the streets that I walked through, dazed at the crowds and activity and scale of the city. It was nostalgic too for Ayman, who grew up not far from here. He pointed out the cinemas where he went to see films with Bruce Lee and Charlie Chan. This is what I love about Ayman; I can see him as a kid. He still has it in him. He took me into a confectioner he used to go to and we ate one of their specialities. It was very good – a syrupy thing topped ingeniously with something between cream and butter to cut the sweetness. We ate it without speaking, just nodding to each other. He said he hadn't been to that place in years.

We walked down Talaat Harb. Ayman pointed out a shop he used to pass when he was a kid from a poor family, wishing he could get his clothes there. I could picture him pressed to the glass, looking in. 'Now I have a fidelity card,' he said, his eyes creasing as he laughed.

The centre had come back to life, after the disturbances. All the shops were open and the street was busy with people. It was as I remembered, only that now there are no police and the vendors have set up stalls on the footpaths and the cars are parked on the street.

We reached Meydan Talaat Harb. Six streets converge here, and the footpath is wider and you can stop and look about without being jostled. Across the road, on a first floor, was a hotel where I had lived in 2005, before I shared the apartment off Mahmoud with Hussein. I had arrived knowing nobody. My experience of the city had been one of pure sensation and, in an attempt to familiarize myself, in however minor a way, with a place that overwhelmed me I had changed hotel every single night. I could not settle, or did not want to. I was like a cat dumped in a strange room, that has to sniff every corner before it can relax. I was not then trying to understand the place. I was simply trying to calm myself enough to breathe it and walk it and see it. I enrolled in a language school so that when I walked through the streets the Arabic script would not be a mystery.

And then I found a room I wanted to stay in – the one I was looking at now with Ayman. It was at the corner of the building, where the turn of about 120 degrees was rounded, so that each of the three windows looked out at Talaat Harb from a slightly different angle. The middle window was a door opening onto a curving balcony. I could close the old wooden shutters, but the chorus of car horns was constant until well after midnight and I fell asleep and woke every day to the sound of the city. The room was empty except for the bed, and I was given a plastic table and plastic chair from the breakfast room, and I sat down at that desk and wrote out a story. The story was about a man and a boy walking down Talaat Harb, not able to understand anything. My priority then was to learn how to deal with hustlers who latched onto you in the street. In the end there was nothing to learn; they can tell by looking at you, by your walk, if you are freshly arrived.

It had got dark, and looking up at that balcony I wanted to go back to that room, and occupy it again, and to sit down and start writing. I felt the room belonged to me, and they would have to give it to me again. I wanted at least to go up there and see it. But I did not give in to the feeling, I just pointed out the balcony to Ayman – it was decorated with twinkling coloured lights – and then he pointed out to me an ice-cream parlour he used to visit, the tip of his finger stained with indelible ink from the polling station.

A land without shortcuts

TIM ROBINSON

This essay originated as the Parnell Lecture, delivered in Magdalene College, Cambridge, in February 2011.

To be summoned to Cambridge from nether Connemara to deliver the Parnell Lecture was a surprise – honorific, but alarming. What to bring, from that famous far-off land? Well, it seems I can begin with good news: the West of Ireland has at last discovered its reason for existing. As you know, Connemara is the land of cloud-shadows drifting across mountainsides. Roundstone, the little fishing and tourist village I live in, is, I claim, the world capital of rainbows. And it has now been discovered that cloud-shadows can be strip-mined, that rainbows can be smelted. For clouds and rain are symptoms of weather, the almost continuous succession of cyclones coming in from the Atlantic, bringing powerful winds, towering waves. Their energy has been going to waste for millions of years, but now it can be tapped; the technology exists, or soon will.

But the trouble with wind energy is that it is never there when you want it. The answer is pumped water storage: use the electricity from forests of wind turbines and shoals of wave-energy converters to pump seawater up into reservoirs in the mountains, and at times of peak demand let it flow down again through generators. And where could one find a landscape better adapted to this grand scheme? In the west of Ireland we have mountains with high glacial valleys, easily dammed, close to an oceanic coastline. These gifts of nature mean that Ireland could not only fuel its own homes and factories but sell the surplus to Europe, exported through a network of pylons and power lines. All this will be unpolluting, greenhouse-gas-free, a noble and profitable Irish contribution to saving the world. An enterprise boldly calling itself 'Spirit of Ireland' is working out the details even now.

In expressing my horror at this vision of the future, I don't want to sound like a climate sceptic. The globe is warming; we are facing into an era of floods, fires, famines; little doubt about it. The Intergovernmental Panel on Climate Change is 95 per cent certain that this is due to human activity. But even if the IPCC authorizes as it were a 5 per cent duty-free allowance of scepticism, I will not avail of it. There is of course intense technical argumentation over the viability of green-energy schemes, but let me take the most sanguine view of them, together with the most anguished view of the environmental crux that seems to make them necessary. The question is, how much of the world do we have to despoil in order to save it? Must we accept armies of jerkily gesticulating giants on our windswept western hills, perpetually drawing attention to themselves, interrupting the flow of horizons, imposing a large common factor of sameness on wonderfully varied landscapes?

The businesses that are set to profit out of a great leap forward in the mechanization of the countryside enjoy a ready justification in terms of energy crises to come. Is there no arguing with their commodification of wilderness's last refuges? A few years ago I flew out to the Aran Islands to participate in a debate on a proposed windfarm there. On the same flight was a vigorous young enthusiast from an alternative technologies firm. When we extricated ourselves from the cramped little flying pram of an aeroplane and stretched ourselves in the island breeze, which carried a thousand miles of ocean and a million wildflowers to our nostrils, he sniffed it and said with delectation, 'Ah! Kilowatt-hours!' We have a so-called Green Party in Ireland devoted to this alternative technology. Seeing it thundering down the road towards us, we would seem to face a choice between two ditches. For the claim that these new modes of energy production are unpolluting is false. Leaving aside the unavoidable pollution caused by their manufacture, transport, installation and decommissioning, they are through their powerful presence grossly disruptive of our aesthetic, corporeal and affective relationships with the Earth. The most obvious component of this loss is that where they go, no one else can go. They mean locked gates, culverted streams, barbed wire, forgone hillsides. These are the spoil-heaps of wind-mining.

How widely applicable are the arguments, or rather the persuasions, I am advancing? Do they stand only on territories comparable in their rare beauty and interest to the ones I have chosen to live amongst? Let no word of mine undermine the stance of those who would defend some superficially unremarkable or already depleted landscape of which they love certain elusive moods and secret places. But I will write in terms of what I know; and let what generalities emerge find their welcome where they can. It has been my joy and privilege over the last third of a century to explore in great detail, to map and to write about three exceptional landscapes – the Aran Islands, the Burren and Connemara – and I will describe a place from each, in search of the qualities we cherish and should protect. Now one might say, 'But surely these famous landscapes are already protected? Is not the Burren a proposed UNESCO World Heritage site?' Well, recently a commercial concern was wooing the people of the Burren with a scheme for pumped seawater storage in a lovely upland valley near Black Head. The idea was not well received locally, and at present planning permission for such a drastic intervention would be hard to obtain – but we are only at the beginning of the alternative industrial revolution as yet, and the statutory designations of parts of these districts as Special Areas of Protection, National Heritage Areas, Geo-parks and so on could someday be swept aside. There are already three wind turbines towering over the otherwise uninterrupted network of ancient field walls on the uninhabited Atlantic side of Inis Meáin in the Aran Islands, constantly crossing themselves as if to ward off the haunting loneliness of the place. And Connemara is repeatedly probed by would-be windfarm developers, who have had a major success recently on its eastern periphery. But I'll not continue with the environmentalist plaint; in fact all I've said so far is just a few swipes of the machete to get me into the centre of the thicket: the nature of place, what makes a place out of a locality, what makes a place so precious that we feel called upon to protect it in the teeth of all rational argumentation.

The Aran Islands first, and in particular the largest of them, Árainn, where I lived in the 1970s. The three islands are fragments of a single limestone escarpment stretching across the mouth of Galway Bay; the villages keep their heads down out of the gales on the north-eastern slopes of the ridge, and on the exposed Atlantic-facing side of the ridge is a literally amazing landscape of stone walls enclosing tiny plots of rough grazing, some of them much overgrown with brambles, some of them hardly more than sheets of bare limestone, their crevices filled with flowering herbs. This side of the island, Na Craga, the crags, is not much visited since farming on the islands is a fading way of life. So the boreens and *roidíní*, the narrow stone-walled paths that wriggle through this maze of fields, are crammed with vegetation. Everywhere, in the spring, are paradisal visions of wildflowers; in my first years there I was drunk on flowers, on the nectar of their names. One day in the course of making my map of the islands I was in such an unfrequented quarter looking for a ruined church I had heard of, one of the many early Christian remains of the islands, nameless and unvisited and abandoned to hazel scrub. A few generations ago, I had been told, an old man called Colm Citte had been passing this way, and had heard the sound of someone churning milk. But he was on his way to Mass, and didn't stop to investigate; he would have been frightened of the fairies in any case. All these places are haunted by half forgotten folktales. The area I am describing now is called Clochán an Airgid, the stone hut of the money, or the silver; there is a *clochán*, an early Christian beehive-shaped hut, which has been reduced to its foundations by treasure hunters following the hint of a legend. Later I wrote about the treasure I found that day, in my book *Stones of Aran*:

As I was crossing the field to the ruins of the church, as obscure as everything else on this occult hillside, I heard through the whispering of the still summer afternoon something that could have been Col Citte's otherworldly churning. Falling water is so rare on Na Craga that I did not identify the sound until I saw a recess under a little scarp at the back of the field, in which silvery drops were cascading through fronds of maidenhair fern and making them tremble continuously. Around this lovely spring were more wildflowers than I had ever gathered in a single glance. On one side of it was a small hawthorn bush with honeysuckle and meadow pea climbing through it, and a lemon-yellow spire of agrimony below, while on the other a tutsan leaned forward to display its flame-coloured berries. Brooklime was growing in the shadow behind the fernleaves, and the other flowers of damp pastures – purple loosestrife, yellow pimpernel, silverweed – mingled with the meadow flowers at my feet – purple clover, kidney-vetch, meadow buttercup, tormentil, birdsfoot trefoil. The stonier slope above the well assembled the flora of the crags at the level of my eyes: burnet rose, bloody cranesbill, mountain everlasting, milkwort, quaking grass, the tiny squinancywort, the last of the early purple orchids and the first of the common spotted orchids, all with a minutely delicate interweaving of fairy flax. Along the foot of the scarp beside the well I could see wild strawberry, scarlet pimpernel, sanicle, the elegant St John's wort. There were tall mulleins flowering on the top of the slope, and twayblades in the shadow of the thickets around the ruin. The band of grey limestone above the well gave it the solemnity of an altar, around which the plants were gathered, each in the colours of its faith. What truth, distilled moment by moment from the rock, was held in perpetual reservation in the dark cup below?

The church behind me, brought to its knees among penitential thorns, attended humbly upon the priestcraft of water.

Re-reading this some fifteen years later, I'm surprised by the salience of the religious terminology. I have no faith, no supernaturalist beliefs; so I must re-examine this. I'll return to the question later.

Strangely, Aran presents this precious conformation of place in three locations, or even more. The reason for this generosity is geological. The island chain is carved out of alternating horizontal strata of limestone and shale – sedimentary rocks laid down in the bed of an ocean that fluctuated in depth over millions of years, the limestone representing times when the water was deep and pure, the shale those when it was shallow and muddy. A central date in this period would be about 325 million years ago. Many millions of years later huge slow earth movements lifted the stacked-up consolidated sediments above sea level, fracturing the brittle limestone, and exposed them to wind, frost, rain, and ice. On the Atlantic-facing coast the waves have licked out the soft shale bands, causing the limestone strata above them to collapse, and so carving sheer or overhanging cliffs. Less abrupt forces of erosion have shaped the more sheltered northeast-facing slopes into a series of broad terraces separated by inland cliffs or scarps ten to twenty feet high. These scarps run along the island chain like contour lines; they each have a stratum of shale usually a few feet deep at their bases, and a thicker stratum of limestone above that. All rainwater quickly sinks through the fractured limestone until it reaches an impervious layer of shale, which channels it horizontally to the foot of one of the little inland scarps, where it bubbles out in springs. Then, flowing out onto the limestone of the terrace below the scarp, it sinks from sight again, only to reappear at the foot of the next scarp, and so on until it reaches the sea. Each of these scarps has a characteristic profile. So the situation I have described, with falling water in a dark recess at the foot of the scarp, a horizontal band of limestone above that, and then a broken slope leading up a few feet to the terrace above, is repeated here and there along the course of the scarp almost from one end of the island to the other. I remember in particular one of my favourite places, reached by walking along a grand level terrace of almost bare limestone behind the house we lived in; it is called An Poll i bhFolach, the hole in hiding. It is most secretively wrapped away in a tiny enclosure between a crooked loop of drystone wall and a nook of the scarp rising from the rock-terrace. A narrow stile in the wall admits one to this fane, or one can scramble down into it from the slopes above by means of a few steps cut into the scarp face. The water lies in a rough stone-lined hollow, reflecting many of the flowers I noted at Clochán an Airgid. This 'hole in hiding' has the apparent self-regard of a place little visited; it welcomes one, then waits for one to go. But human industry has intensified its mode of being; there was always a spring here, brought forth by the hydrology I have described; then the wall was built round it to stop wandering cattle trampling it into mud, and the stile and the steps provided for people fetching water from it to their beasts in nearby fields. This is a centripetal place; it draws one in and precludes the outward view. At its focus is the glint of the water that shows itself briefly before disappearing again into the earth.

There is another well a mile or so away, at the foot of the same scarp as An Poll i bhFolach and the well of Clochán an Airgid, and therefore strikingly similar to it in the formation of the cliffy slope above it. And here the mystery of water, its life-giving powers, is explicitly celebrated, for this is a holy well. In fact it is the well that inspired J.M. Synge's play *The Well of the Saints*. Its legend is the familiar one of the miraculous cure of blindness; Synge himself recorded it during his first visit to the islands, in 1898. A woman living in Sligo who had a blind son dreamed of the well and the cure in its waters, and took a boat and brought her son to Aran. She declined all guidance from the locals and went straight to the well, prayed, bathed her son's eyes – and saw his face fill with joy as he exclaimed over the beauty of the flowers around the well. This well is beside one of the islands' most beautiful little medieval chapels, Teampall an Cheathrair Álainn, the Church of the Beautiful Four. These comely persons are by ancient sources identified as Saints Fursey, Brendan of Birr, Conall and Berchan; but I do not vouch for the historicity of their presence here. It is fitting that legend names this well as Tobar an Cheathrair Álainn, the Well of the Beautiful Four, for beauty is the characteristic I want to retain from the handful of places I have plucked out of the Aran Islands. Now I'll go in search of a place with a different essence.

After I had made my map of the Aran Islands I looked around me, and there to the east on the mainland were the silver-grey uplands of the Burren. This is limestone country too, of heavily glaciated karst, with fertile valleys hidden from each other by rounded or terraced hills of bare, fissured, rock-sheets. It is rich in prehistoric remains; within say 150 square miles, there are sixty-six megalithic tombs and over four hundred circular enclosures ranging from ruinous but still mighty triple-ramparted cashels to slight walls that once enclosed the stockyards of humble farmsteads. Many of these monuments are almost drowned in thousands of acres of hazel scrub. To force myself into every corner of this daunting territory I decided to visit all the ancient sites marked on the old six-inch-to-the-mile Ordnance Survey maps that were my template, and in so doing I found many more antiquities. But it was a long, lonely struggle, often in foul weather. It is often claimed that the Burren is a spiritual landscape, but if so it harbours an obstructive, secretive spirit among others, one that stretches brambles across paths, makes rock slippery with rain and confounds horizons with mist. Once, as I stood in the rain in a roofless church ruin, up to my knees in wet nettles, I was shown the severed head of a statue of a bishop, by an old man who seemed quite ready to demonstrate its use as a cursing-stone by turning it anticlockwise and so inflicting a stroke or a drowning on some enemy. Suddenly I felt a revulsion against the Burren, its obscurantist myths, its labyrinthine refusal to provide an intelligible view of itself, its slithery resistance to the grip of cartography. At other times its breezy, sunny hillsides, mobile with wildflowers and butterflies, were annexes to heavenly skies. And most frequently it drifted between these extremes, moody, ambiguous, as in the place I am going to describe.

A narrow road leads up out of one of the valleys of the central Burren onto a bleak plateau; I often had to push my bike up and across it. Scanning the plateau one sees an apparently endless recession of fields separated by breast-high drystone walls enclosing little but grey rock riven by fissures full of brambles and bracken. A solitary wind-inflected thorn tree and a deserted single-storey farmhouse show on the horizon. The monotony of this area challenged me. There must be something hidden among these countless walls, I felt, something I can rescue from the nullity, the sterility, of mere location and mark on my map – for it is the attention we bring to it that makes a place out of a location. I used to leave my bike by the road and spend time straying to and fro among these anonymous fields. I never met anyone there. Then I came across a field that seemed worth recording, not for anything in it – the usual wind-shorn shaggy thistly stuff lurking in every crevice – but for the walls enclosing it. In many parts of the Burren it is easy to prise up large thin slabs out of the topmost layer of rock; the builders of megalithic tombs did it, and in Aran, which shares the geology of the Burren, the making of tombstones out of such slabs, and selling them to the south Connemara folk who do not live on limestone but on granite, was a thriving industry in the nineteenth century.

Limestone is of course vulnerable to erosion; it is eaten away by the carbonic acid in rainwater, and any crack that water can penetrate will be enlarged over the centuries into a crevice many inches wide. Sometimes these crevices develop into gullies and basins of fantastic shapes. And this field had been fenced with slabs set on edge that exhibited – the word is right – a great variety of amoeboid piercings that would have pleased the surrealist sculptor Hans Arp. Look through these weird windows, and what is on one side is as lugubriously anonymous as what is on the other. I wanted to put this field on my map, but of course there was no way of indicating what was remarkable about it on the map sheet; nor did I want to make too much of it in a land of such marvels as the Burren. In the end I marked it with a dot and in tiny print the words 'a strange field'. Occasionally I hear from someone who has noticed this cartographic curiosity and gone in search of its objective correlative. Usually they have been unsure whether or not they found what I had found, or what it was they were supposed to see in it – but then there is nothing to be seen in it, just grey emptiness, nodding thistles, an occasional attendance of puzzled visitors on a mystique. I take from this instance another modality of places: strangeness.

From our little house perched on the skyline of Árainn we could look out across ten miles of sea to the ragged peninsulas and archipelagos of Connemara and its core of mountains. Nothing of the orderly levels of limestone here, instead an arrested flux and turbulence of upended and overthrown strata half quenched in a coastline of baffling intricacy. To map it seemed a reasonable conclusion to what already had become a totally unreasonable project of mapping all the land I could see from my home – as if I were so far lost that only a comprehensive universal map would find my place. At first my plan was merely to map that unmappably complex southern coastline, which I set out to walk from end to end, peninsula by peninsula, island after island, over a number of sessions of a few weeks each. This task, which seemed to impose itself like a ritual obligation of obscure significance, took so long that in the end we decided to move to the mainland and extend the map to include the mountains and the western, Atlantic, coast of Connemara as well. I was several years into this project when I came across the place I am going to select for description, out of Connemara's fecundity of place.

Gleann Eidhneach, the ivied glen, leads up into the centre of the cluster of mountains called the Twelve Pins. In the last Ice Age a glacier nested on a sunless north-facing slope of the mountain massif, and as it grew and inched downhill under its own weight it gouged out this wide flat-bottomed valley as a way for itself, before joining other glaciers coming down out of other mountain dens, and eventually finding its way to the sea. Ten or twelve thousand years ago it melted back, dumping thousands of tons of clay and boulders, a moraine that now lies like a rampart across the valley floor. A vigorous stream meandering down the valley has breached these drifts and flows through a little canyon twenty or thirty feet deep. Thousands of years of bog growth have carpeted the valley with heather and rounded the forms of the glacial moraine; bare rock shows only on the mountain slopes on either side.

The place I would describe is perched on the smooth back of the moraine. I noticed it for the first time when walking up the valley in company of an ornithologist; we were going to look for raven and peregrine falcon nests on the precipice at the head of the valley. We stopped to rest for a moment, and, idly looking before me across the valley, I saw six little vertebrae sticking up from the spine of the moraine, that aroused my curiosity. We splashed across a couple of hundred yards of wet bog and ran up onto the moraine, where we found a line of small boulders – a stone alignment in fact, a type of monument usually dated to the Bronze Age. The boulders were of the local quartzite; the largest, at the southern end of the row, was about waist high and contained a good deal of white quartz. I did not take much notice of the direction in which they were aligned – at first glance the row seemed to be pointing vaguely at the mountain wall on the south side of the valley. But when the trained archaeologists came along to verify my report of this find, one of them – Michael Gibbons – noticed that in fact it pointed at a V-shaped cleft in the high skyline, a high mountain pass leading over into the next valley. Further, he came back to the site on the shortest day of the year, the day of the winter solstice, when the sun's arc is at its lowest and the point at which it sets is at its southerly extreme – and found that, as observed from the stone alignment, the sun staged its farewell to the year exactly in that cleft. The following midwinter I went up the valley to pay my respects to this phenomenon. At two o'clock of the short winter afternoon the sun was blazing, but it was already in the grip of the mountains. Every minute detail of the northern side of the valley, with its little potato plots straggling up the steeps from two isolated farmhouses, was gold-washed, while the southern mountain wall was in deep shade. The last of the sunbeams were so intense that, looking along the alignment into the dazzlement, it was hard to make out what was happening. As the sun slipped slowly down into the cleft its radiance seemed to erode the profiles of the slopes on either side. The flecks of white quartz in the stones of the alignment almost leaped from their beds in the flood of energy. Then the sun was gone and the great mountain shadows stretched out across the valley floor. The longest night was beginning; beyond that, the spring was already in waiting, and all the annual phenomena of concern to the Bronze Age folk who had wrestled those boulders into position on the crest of the moraine: the passage of migrating geese, the warmth necessary for sowing corn, the salmons' ascent of the stream. The calendar started from this day, to which the alignment pointed as certainly as Christian spires point to heaven.

But why was that alignment built exactly where it was? For, if you think of it, as the setting sun moved across the sky, the mountain shadow with the cleft in its profile must have swept across quite an extent of the valley floor, so that there would have been many other points from which it would appear that the sun was setting into the cleft; an alignment in any of these places would function just as well as the actual one as the focus of a ritual or to mark the point from which the solstitial sunset was to be observed by some priest-astronomer of the valley community. But then the crest of the moraine is in itself a proud place: it commands the valley floor, it stands its ground in the face of the encircling mountains. If the spring wells I described from the Aran Islands are centripetal places, this Connemara site is centrifugal: vision is spun out from it, its mode of placehood is that of the outlook, the point of view. (Such observations belong to a field of study one could call distemics, the phenomenology of far-off things.)

But there is one defect in this grand spectacle of the solstitial sunset: the sun doesn't quite reach the bottom of the cleft in the horizon before disappearing behind the mountain to the west of it. If the stone alignment were a little further south, or the arc of the sun's passage across the sky were a little lower, the effect would be perfect, and even more dramatic. But consider this: the daily journeying of the sun from east to west is of course the effect of the earth's turning on its axis. A spinning top appears to bow in all directions, as every child notices; the orientation of its axis changes slowly, sweeping out a cone; the phenomenon is called precession, I remember from my mathematical days. So too for the earth, with complications – nutations, or noddings – due to its equatorial paunch, to the pull of the moon and the other planets; the upshot of these influences being that the angle of the earth's axis to the plane of its orbit round the sun changes cyclically by about two and a half degrees, with a period of 41,000 years. This angle is currently decreasing, so that the midwinter sun seems to pass across the sky perhaps half a degree higher than it did say 3,500 years ago. So the Bronze Agers got their celestial architecture exactly right. In their day the midwinter sun, as seen from the stone alignment, disappeared precisely into the bottom of the cleft in the mountain skyline. (When I say 'precisely' and 'exactly', I am of course writing with the degree of precision one would expect of a row of boulders, rather than of a sextant.)

Making this mental correction to the spectacle of the midwinter sunset feels like adjusting the focus of an optical instrument, which is what the alignment, taken together with the cleft in the skyline, really is. From this perfectly placed place on the top of the moraine, a panorama of the mountain walls and the wide wild glen offers itself, and on the shortest day of midwinter another perspective opens up like the aperture in the dome of an observatory; one can see halfway to infinity and eternity, not only the dazzling millions of miles to the sun but the three or four thousand years back to the Bronze Age, and the forty-one-thousand-year wobble of the earth's tilted axis. The place is a foothold on a globe that is tumbling through space and time. The prehistoric links us back to the cosmic. Antiquity is the term I'll take to embrace both.

Do the virtually limitless depths of antiquity nullify our concerns with the present and the near future? Our barricades against global warming, whatever form they take, are hardly likely to be visible in the landscape in a few centuries' time. Also, we human beings have discovered a way of looking at time as if it were all spread out before us like the Bayeux tapestry, and the comprehensiveness of this vision consoles us for the narrowness of the segment of the panorama representing our own lifetimes. Nevertheless, like any other animal, each of us is the embodied origin of a particular perspective on time and space: what is near and soon concerns us with the urgency of a life we feel flowing away from us even as we live it. We are inescapably at the sharp end of this outlook, whether it extends into deep time or not. The tapestry model of time offers meagre protection; we can bundle it into a wad to blunt the point but we are still impaled upon the perspectives that constitute us.

Beauty, strangeness, antiquity – three fragile moments of place. The places I have described may stand for all the delicate facets of the Earth that make it the jewel of the known cosmos. None of the places I have conjured up for you out of the Aran Islands, the Burren and Connemara are in present danger. But you can imagine how a wind turbine up on that lonely plateau of the Burren would suck all the strangeness out of it and mince it up, and how the stone alignment and its literally spectacular relationship to topography and cosmology would fare if that magnificent valley were to be dammed to store up the 'Spirit of Ireland'. On the Aran Islands, with the decline of cattle farming and the increase of building, a little unofficial quarry could obliterate a place like An Poll i bhFolach overnight; in fact the ravishingly beautiful well of Clochán an Airgid had a narrow escape from such a fate during our time on the island. And we are only at the beginning of society's reaction to the threat of global warming. What will be the pressures on us in a decade or two? Will irresolution be replaced by panic? For we have read dire predictions. Breach the recommended two-degree limit to global warming and we trigger a runaway process of positive feedback; at six degrees, say some of the experts, the vast quantities of methane safely tucked away on the ocean bed come boiling to the surface and ignite in a worldwide fireball. If anything like that happened, the Earth would surely be screaming to be rid of us. Clearly we cannot be party to the extermination of all higher life, whatever it costs to avert it. And on the current modes of calculating that cost, the West of Ireland, whatever its stores of beauty, strangeness and antiquity, would be sacrificed. In which case what I have said about my three paradigms of place can be heard as an elegy for all lost places. I want to raise our awareness of what is at stake to a level approaching pain, a pre-emptive nostalgia for the places we love – and nothing sharpens the sensibilities so much as the threat of loss.

But the die is not yet cast. There is still time for a redirected human will, informed by a truly alternative set of values, to divert the course of events. So let my three descriptions be heard instead as a call to the defence of such places. And there is a special rightness in raising this call as from the west of Ireland, for a cult of place, or at least of placenames, is traceable in Irish culture from earliest times down to the present. The foundation myth of this cult is preserved in the medieval Irish text *Acallam na Senórach*, the Colloquy of the Elders. This compilation of stories concerning Fionn mac Cumhal and his warrior band the Fianna has as its framing device a wandering around

Ireland undertaken by St Patrick in the company of Caílte, one of Fionn's band who has somehow long outlived his companions and is now submitting himself to the new order symbolized by the coming of the saint. At each of the forts and prominent landscape features they pass, Caílte pronounces its name and recites the events – usually bloody and uncanny – from which the name derives, and St Patrick commands one of his scribes to write them down for the edification of futurity. Thus the work enacts the passing-on of the Celtic Iron Age placelore to the Christian dispensation – and although the text as it has come down to us is a product of monastic scriptoria it is filled with a sense of yearning for the great old days when the hunters revelled in the sights and sounds of the forest and the hills, and the doors of the otherworld lay open everywhere. Dinnsheanchas, as it is called, the lore of place, the exegesis of placenames, is a persistent feature of Irish literature, down to Brian Friel's *Translations*, in which a young British officer engaged in the first Ordnance Survey of Ireland in the 1830s, and an Irish peasant girl, having no common language, exchange as love-gifts recitations of the placenames each of them has grown up amongst.

However, it must be admitted that this Irish fascination with placenames is too often purely nominal and does not extend to caring for the places themselves; nostalgia stands in for conservation and convenience trumps all. Here's an evocative list of placenames from a public notice I saw in a newspaper a few years ago. They are the names of townlands, the small land divisions that often equate to a single farmhouse and its land, or a hamlet, or a stretch of commonage:

Doughiska, Garraun North, Coolagh, Glennascaul, Frenchfort, Carnmore, Lisheenkyle, Barrettes Park, Caherbriskaun, Carraun Duff, Rathmorrissy, Pollnagroagh, Ballygarraun, Newford, Prospect, Baunmore, Gartnahoon, Furzypark, Farranablake, Boyhill, Toberconnolly, Loobroe, Moyode, Deerpark, Rathgorgin, Esker, Brusk, Carragh More,

Greyford, Kiltullagh, Clogharevaun, Carrowroe, Ballynahown, Bookeen, Carrowkeel, Clashagranny, Knocknaduala, Galboley, Carrowreagh, Killescragh, Caraun More, Cross, Cloonconaun, Rahally, Slievedotia, Brackloon, Rathglass, Owenavaddy, Treanbaun, Ballymabilla, Toormore, Gortnahoon, Cappataggle, Ballynaclogh, Slihaun Beg, Cloghagalla Oughter, Cloghagalla Eighter, Cooltymurraghy, Cloonameragaun, Coololla, Curragh, Barnacragh, Liscappul, Loughbown, Mackney, Garbally Demesne, Brackemagh, Moher, Dunlo, Pollboy, Tulrush, Ardcarn, Suckfield, Kilgarve, Beagh.

I wrote out this list as part of a letter to the *Irish Times* in 2004, suggesting that its readers might relish it. And I ended by saying:

> I don't know these little places, but I am sure they are as rich in variety and individuality as their names are, even in these anglicised forms. But this is the list of townlands to be torn through by the proposed N6 dual carriageway from Ballinasloe to Galway.
>
> Read the list again, and weep.

But that was in boom-time Ireland, the Old Woman of the Four Green-Field Sites. The paper did not publish my letter, and nobody wept. In fact from visitors to Connemara I hear nothing but praise of the new road, which reduces the driving time down from Dublin to three hours or so; and indeed if I had to do that journey often I'd feel the same. Ours is the age of the shortcut, trading space for time; technology is shortcuts, ever bridging the gap between intent and fulfilment. And, technology having hurried us into the present crux of global warming, it now offers to deliver us from it, in return for the ground from beneath our feet. But before we sacrifice the 'hole in hiding' (taking that tender spot in the Aran Islands to stand for all the places liable to be brushed aside by the renewable-energy industries) there is much we can and should give up, if necessary by going the long way round, by abjuring some of the shortcuts of technology. I might suggest that war, the ultimate (but often delusive) technological shortcut in its impatient abandonment of the serpentine ways of diplomacy, is a luxury of which we could be sparing. (In discussion of the rights and wrongs of current and recent wars I don't remember seeing their carbon footprints mentioned, although they must be gigantic.) But I don't feel called upon to design the carbon-frugal, place-conserving economy we need; that's for the experts, including right-minded technologists. However, perhaps I can say something about the re-evaluation of place that might motivate such a project.

First, the role of placenames. Reverting to that list of places knocked about by the new dual carriageway: they are given in their anglicized forms, but in most cases one can recognize the original Irish-language versions underlying them. These are both musical and meaningful. Dabhach Uisce, water hole; Lisín Coille, little fort of the wood; Baile an Gharráin, the village of the thicket; Gort na hUamhna, field of the cave; Eiscir – an *eiscir* is a ridge of glacial deposits marking the course of a river that flowed under the ice of the last glaciation; Sliabh Dóite, burnt mountain; Ceapach an tSeagal, the rye plot; Clocha Gealla, bright stones; Lios Capaill, ringfort of the horse … all pregnant with history and topography. To idealize a linguistic situation that in reality is often ravaged and corrupted, a placename summarizes the place's attributes and origins, asserts its excellencies and rights to respect. Therefore the handing down and rehearsal of its placename is a place's first defence against neglect or exploitation, against its being regarded as a mere shortcut to some other more profitable place. Among the historical roots of Ireland's carelessness of place is the retreat of its language and the accompanying anglicization of its placenames, which have been defaced, rendered dumb and sometimes reduced to the ridiculous. To undo a little of this damage has been for me, an Englishman, a work of reparation.

One reason I have found the placenames of Connemara and the Aran

Islands so fascinating is that they are for the most part in the Irish that is still current, and that my access to the language is limited, so that they appear to me as so many secrets to be unveiled, riddles to be solved, clues to a mystery, passwords to a cult. And with the word 'cult', a tinge of the religious comes in again. What might a cult of place entail? One could take guidance from the ancient cult of holy wells – with which I have become very familiar, my map of Connemara being constellated with the dozens of holy wells I have been shown, many of them known only to a few old folk of the immediate vicinity. The cult involves visiting, thoughtfulness, ritual handling of pebbles, water, flowers – as well as features we can do without: superstition, penitential barefootedness, repetitive mumblings. A secular version might call forth an awareness of the place's constitution, the causal net that brought it into existence, from cosmic origins to the casual touch of local microhistory. On such occasions the basic act of attention that creates a place out of a location would be renewed, enhanced by whatever systems of understanding we can muster, from the mathematical to the mythological, by the passion of poetry, or by simple enjoyment of the play of light on it. Here is a gateway to a land without shortcuts, where each place is bathed in the sunlight of our contemplation and all its particularities brought forth, like those mountainside potato plots gilded by midwinter sunset in the valley of the stone alignment.

I bring this suggestion forward with some hesitation, being uncomfortably aware that to propose the cult of holy wells as a model for our times might appear quaint, hopelessly antiquated, terminally rustic. Have I sojourned too long in Connemara? But, reading through the descriptions of the three places I have given you, I note that in each case I have spontaneously drawn on imagery of pilgrimage and shrine. Realizing that the mindful seeking-out of place has been the half-subconscious drive of my practice in all these years of mapping and topographical writing, I can hardly disown this terminology now, unbeliever though I be. And since for centuries the material world was seen as a quarry of metaphors to describe the glories of a spiritual world, that gorgeous structure of the imagination should in return provide the liturgy and ceremonial we need for a praiseful approach to the places that glorify the here below.

Placenames, whether they exist in the mind of the Irish *seanchaí*, the custodian of traditional lore, or in the memory banks of a database, are only the anchor points of a discourse of place. To create a language for the secular celebration of the Earth, with the height and power of the religious tradition but purged of supernaturalism, can be seen as the task of ecoliterature, tracked and made conscious of itself by ecocriticism. But can literature submit to being welded to any particular aim or study in the way these awkwardly compounded terms suggest? A better word might be 'geophany', with its echo of theophany, the manifestation of a deity, or the celebration of such an appearance. If I have to call on the terminology of religion it is because that is the language evolved to address the highest; and the highest is what lies under our feet and bears us up. Geophany, then, the showing forth of the Earth through all the geophanic arts and sciences, should be our means towards a reformation of values. The secretive beauty of Aran's spring wells, the strangeness of the ragged little fields of the Burren, the deep antiquity of the stone alignment in Connemara, stand here for the countless precious things for which we will be mourning, if in ten or twenty years' time we find we have sacrificed them to the technology of shortcuts, in a misdirected effort to save the world.

Boom tomb

DONALD MAHONEY

In mid January I travelled by bus from Ennis, in Co. Clare, to Achill Island, off the coast of Co. Mayo, a journey of 120 miles that took all day. I had great aspirations that day to make a dent in Sebald's *Austerlitz*, but after reading the following passage, near the Galway–Mayo border – 'somehow we know by instinct that outsize buildings cast the shadow of their own destruction before them, and are designed from the first with an eye to their later existence as ruins' – I started to feel nauseated and closed the book. I listened to two old women who'd travelled to Galway to get their hair done speak knowingly about the residents of almost every house along the N60 until we reached Castlebar. The thirty-eight-mile last leg – Westport to Achill – took two hours. Pensioners got off at the side of the road and disappeared up driveways towards unlit bungalows. The darkness that night in western Mayo was absolute. No stars, no moon, no streetlights, no houses on the horizon.

My purpose in going to Achill was to investigate the massive circular structure erected in late November 2011 by the property developer Joe McNamara. McNamara, who reportedly owes €3.5 million to Anglo Irish Bank, first came to public attention when he parked a cement mixer with the words 'Anglo Toxic Bank' painted on its side at the gates of Dáil Éireann in September 2010; three months later he abandoned a cherry picker with its arm extended into the sky and its radio blaring Morricone's *The Good, the Bad and the Ugly* soundtrack on Kildare Street. He was born and raised on Achill, and the site he'd chosen for his grandest provocation was a scenic boggy hilltop about five miles from the western tip of the island. Photos taken at daybreak of the concrete ring appeared on the front page of the *Irish Times* and in the *Irish Independent*, and some cultural commentators declared it to be a work of art. Like many pieces of large-scale public art commissioned over the past twenty-five years – Anthony Gormley's *Angel of the North* being proba-bly the best known – McNamara's structure, to judge by photographs, attempted to enact a dramatic reimagining of the landscape. But Achillhenge, as it came to be known because of its rough resemblance to Stonehenge, was not commissioned by a local authority. It was built over a weekend on commonage, without planning permission. Mayo County Council quickly secured an injunction from the High Court to have construc-tion stopped; McNamara would spend four days in Mountjoy prison for refusing to halt work on the structure. He applied to Mayo County Council for a Section 5 planning exemption, claiming that what he had created was an ornamental garden, but the application was refused in mid January. The council's application to the High Court for an order to demolish the structure had not been adjudicated at the time of writing. Among many other things, I hoped a visit to Achill might explain why McNamara had gone to the trouble.

The Annexe, the only pub trading in Keel during winter, was my first port of call. Before ordering a pint, I had to announce myself and my intentions to the bar. It was January, after all, and strangers were thin on the ground. 'Just off the bus. Here for the weekend. Hoping to see the henge.' The men at the bar spoke freely of the structure and provided me with directions to it but no one mentioned its architect by name. I hoped that people might open up after a few drinks, but McNamara was clearly not a subject of discussion, at least not with outsiders. I asked Marty, the barman, how the pub got its unusual name. 'Because that's what it was called a hundred years ago,' he responded curtly.

I headed out for Achillhenge the next morning, walking west from Keel along the island's main road, towards the villages of Pollagh and Dooagh. Clusters of bungalows, most of them empty, lined the road. Planning permis-sion notices had been posted near the front gates of many of them. To the south, Achill's desolate beauty extended itself. Minaun, a monstrous mound of rock, rose out of Keel Bay, and behind her were the imposing Mweelin cliffs.

McNamara had promised 'no more protests' after charges of dangerous driving in relation to the cherry-picker incident were withdrawn last May, but the Achill project involved months of planning. Acquaintances of the family were warned of 'something big' during the summer of 2011. Work began on Achillhenge during the last weekend in November. The concrete had been cast in Galway and was transported up to Achill on thirty large low-loaders. The low-loaders were stationed at the car park of the Achill Head Hotel, McNamara's listed address on the island, which was about a quarter mile from the site where the structure would be built. Achill natives saw the fleet and wondered what McNamara was up to. The woman who ran the B&B where I stayed guessed he was building windmills. He employed five people during the construction process: a welder, a crane driver, and three men to drive the low-loaders.

Just after St Patrick's church, I came to a small sign that said 'Achillhenge', painted in white on black slate, pointing uphill at Mary's Lane. There were ore hand-painted signs along the way, guiding walkers towards the new attraction and away from private roads. At a junction, I encountered a black sheepdog who led me past an orange house with children playing in the front yard and then past two identical unlived-in houses, a large shed and a red Daewoo sedan with four flat tires. The paved road gave way to something muddier. Soon I caught my first glimpse of Achillhenge, framed by two massive piles of earth.

The structure comprises 120 slabs of concrete. Three slabs had been cast together to create each of the ring's thirty columns, standing about twelve feet in height and positioned at intervals of about four feet in a circle of about a hundred feet in diameter. Thirty smaller lintel slabs were laid horizontally on top of the columns, creating thirty portals.

McNamara did not simply plant Achillhenge on the land. His team dug about five feet into the ground, through a top layer of grass, then some buttery, boggy topsoil, and finally into layers of earth and limestone. A foundational circular road was paved so the low-loaders could operate and the structure could be erected. The earth was discarded casually around the site, and now forms an outer ring that is as tall as the structure in places. In the untidy state it was left in, Achillhenge echoed the layout of many Neolithic earthwork henges, which are defined by a raised bank and a flattened ditch. The land itself is commonage, though McNamara claimed his family had a right to build on the site.

It was impossible not to marvel at the structure. It looked unshakeable. It had clearly been inspired by Stonehenge, but it had an eerie contemporaneity because it was made of cold, cheap concrete. A hillwalker who knew nothing of Joe McNamara might stumble upon Achillhenge and presume it was the skeleton of an audacious summer house. But its circularity suggested something monumental. Perhaps it was, as one man on the island put it, a 'boom tomb'.

McNamara's solicitor described the structure to the High Court as a 'place of reflection'. A report in the *Mayo News* cited 'sources close to the Achill native' as saying that McNamara 'had designed and planned the towering structure so that it would align with the solstices – on June 21 and December 21. The sun would rise on those mornings over the mountains in Achill and shine through one of the gaps in the outer ring and light up a centre-piece.' It seems unlikely, given the design of the structure, that such an effect would be confined to the two solstices; in any case, the county council intervened before the centrepiece could be erected. Instead, the middle of the ring is covered in mud and rock, bar the odd undisturbed tuft of grass.

The site on which McNamara built would have been an ideal position from which to view the stunning scenery around the west of Achill – Slievemore, Achill's highest mountain; Minaun; Keel Bay and its minor islands; the vast Atlantic; acres upon acres of unspoiled commonage and what looked like the turret of an ancient castle beyond the north-westerly horizon – but viewed from within the structure the landscape is reduced to a series of framed, muddled vantage points. I tried to turn my thoughts inwards, but this was made difficult by the inane graffiti on many of the stones: 'Arse!', 'TITS ARE GREAT!', 'Balls, Love It!', 'Wot do you think?', 'SLAB'. Three games of tic-tac-toe had been played and a CCTV camera had been drawn with a black marker.

Flaws in the structure became more apparent upon closer inspection. The slab resting on the column bearing the 'TITS' graffito, for instance, sat unevenly, at an angle of about ten degrees. Metal support beams that had been laid horizontally under the cement bank had emerged from the ground in places.

Two months after its construction, public curiosity about Achillhenge was still strong: nine other people visited the site during the two hours I spent there. They were of different ages, and all spent about fifteen or twenty minutes observing the structure as if it were something you might find in an art gallery. A video filmed on a blustery afternoon and uploaded to YouTube on 5 December shows two teenagers walking its circumference atop the lintel slabs. There's no evidence of how they managed to mount the structure, but the footage captures a few gusty moments of Achill's raw beauty.

Achillhenge sits exposed on high ground, and a bitter south-easterly wind (which someone would later describe as 'summery') left me freezing. I headed back to Keel to explore McNamara's other building projects on the island. About a mile from Achillhenge, you'll find a Celtic Tiger burial pit of the sort that you'd expect to encounter on the fringes of a midlands town. A quiet pub called the Village Inn had once stood there, and McNamara bought the site and had the pub knocked. He'd planned to build a hotel, then tried to change the planning permission so that the size of the hotel could be increased; this application was unsuccessful, and work stalled. McNamara had borrowed the money for the job from Anglo Irish Bank. This was 2006;

the work would never be finished. The site stretched about a hundred metres from the main road towards the sea, and was dug about twenty feet into the earth. When I visited, a large cement mixer sat rusting, visible from the road. Most of the ground had been paved and metal support beams jutted out of the cement in groups of five and six, forming a grid. Layers of fencing, covered with green mesh and rope, had been placed to keep people out, and were bordered by parking barriers along the roadside. If it had been completed, the hotel would have had remarkable views of Minaun and the nearby beach. Instead it was not so much an eyesore as a void. Someone in the Annexe suggested relocating Achillhenge onto this site.

In Barrett's CostCutter in Keel, I noticed that thirty people had signed a petition to save Achillhenge. Achill's population is 2,700, and I'm still not sure if the petition reflected rousing support or indifference. The media have portrayed McNamara as something of a heroic outsider artist – Achillhenge was pitched for the Turner Prize and described as a 'Reason to be Cheerful' in the *Irish Times* in December – while a *Mayo News* report from the site on a cloudy winter solstice morning suggested that McNamara had the power to make the sun come out: 'There was a feeling that nothing was impossible. Not with Joe McNamara involved.' I got a slightly different impression on Achill. Most of the people I talked to spoke with a sort of awe at the brazenness of the undertaking of Achillhenge, but in the same breath would politely ask me if I'd seen the site in Keel. Some people were surprised at the media's positive portrayal of Achillhenge. One man I spoke to likened McNamara's national public profile to that of James Lynchehaun, an Achill native who, after being arrested for beating and disfiguring Agnes McDonnell, a landlord for whom he worked as an agent, in 1894, escaped from custody and hid out on the island for months, becoming something of a legend in the process. J.M. Synge heard the story during his visits to Achill and partly based Christy Mahon in *The Playboy of the Western World* on Lynchehaun. Perhaps our desperate need for a rebel during this time of national shame has distorted our assessments of McNamara, a property developer with an interest in pre-Christian spirituality and a fondness for concrete.

The next day, I decided to revisit Achillhenge. This time I took a shortcut overland from my B&B. There were few boundaries on the land, and the fences that did exist had been kicked over in places. The ground was marshy and I started to doubt my own footing. Step wrongly and the black earth itself would swallow me whole, or so it seemed. The only other living creature I encountered was a startled hare. Eventually, I joined the old train-line road and followed it towards the top of a hill that surveyed the western tip of Achill, with the sea beyond it and Clare Island at the edge of the horizon, looking like a pregnant woman lying on her back. From that vantage point, McNamara's ring took on a magical quality. The sun had cracked though the clouds and a thin layer of mist had settled around the ring. Seen from a certain distance, Achillhenge seemed to mirror the timelessness of the mountains and the sea.

I continued my approach overland, passing some fenced-in bog and an abandoned grey car about a quarter mile from any driveable road. Its windows were smashed and its seats were ripped up. The ground got wetter and wetter. I climbed a tall mound of earth that put me at eye-level with the top of the structure. Someone had climbed Achillhenge in the twenty-four hours since my last visit and left two small cairns atop it. There was new graffiti as well: 'Ná scriostear é!' and 'Teach Solais'. Five children had signed their names.

The purpose of the enterprise remained unclear. Surely McNamara expected the Mayo County Council to do everything in its power to make sure Achillhenge was not allowed to stand. But even if the High Court was to render it a 'temporary installation' (to borrow the language of contemporary art), McNamara had made a mark on the land that would take years and years to cover up. Many on the island doubted that the county council had the logistical and financial ability to remove the structure. I departed feeling that despite the fascinating things it does to and within the landscape, and the public interest it has generated, Achillhenge is first and foremost a monument to its creator. In its disrespect for the law and the environment, it embodies the spirit of feckless development that has crippled Ireland.

An older woman and a teenage girl were doing a lap of the ring as I prepared to leave. 'I hope they keep it,' the older woman said as she passed me.

At the southern base of Slievemore there is an abandoned village, and I decided to explore it in the two hours I had to kill before my bus left. En route, I passed a house that McNamara had built for himself. It, too, was unfinished, though it looked inhabitable from the outside. Most of the houses on Achill were white bungalows, but this was a two-storey villa clad in ostentatious orange brick, with verandas looking out towards Minaun. Its most striking feature was the imposing wall at the front of the property, which stood about ten feet high and was topped in places by metal railings with arrowhead-shaped tops. The wall also featured odd circular and semi-circular brick arrangements – more evidence, perhaps, of McNamara's aesthetic.

I reached the abandoned village half an hour later. It was beside the island's graveyard. From afar, it looked like a field exposed limestone, but as I approached I could see the foundations of houses. A sign said it was called The Abandoned Village because nobody knew its original name. Heinrich Böll had lived nearby in Dugort and had written about the village in his *Irish Journal*: 'No bombed city, no artillery-raked village ever looked like this, for bombs and shells are nothing but extended tomahawks, battle-axes, maces, with which to smash, to hack to pieces, but here there is no trace of violence; in limitless patience time and the elements have eaten away everything not made of stone, and from the earth have sprouted cushions on which these bones lie like relics, cushions of moss and grass.' Even in Böll's time on Achill, more than fifty years ago, there was confusion about what had happened to the village and its people. 'No one could tell us exactly when and why the village had been abandoned,' he wrote.

A man in his twenties, finishing his descent of Slievemore, stopped to talk to me outside the village. I asked him how high he had to climb to see Achillhenge. He pointed to one of the mountain's uppermost ridges. From that height, it didn't seem to have made much of an impression on him.

The bridge that links Achill to the mainland is not long. The tide was out when my bus drove over it and a narrow channel of shallow water divided the island from the rest of Mayo. The only people on the bus were myself, the mountain-climber and a middle-aged man with rosary beads wrapped around his wrists. I watched the scenery pass and tried to imagine some point in the future, generations from now, when Ireland's economic collapse was a matter of history, no longer a reality to be negotiated daily. Perhaps Achillhenge will be viewed, like the deserted village, as just another Achill ruin. The power of its presence may grow. I remembered a conversation I had had with a woman in Lourdie's pub in Dooagh on Saturday night. She had been walking towards Achillhenge along the old train tracks with a friend. As the structure appeared on the horizon, she said to him: 'What will they say about it a few hundred years from now? What will it say about us?'

'Twenty-first-century concrete,' her friend replied.

Extravagances

ANTHONY CALESHU

It's probably best to begin with the moment we became aware of him, her husband, in the doorway of the room. I think it was she who noticed him first, standing there in his suit, with the frozen look a child might have if, from the window, say, his bedroom window, he saw his mother outside being beaten by the mailman. She said his name, 'Gil', as if even his name surprised her.

'Gil!' she said, from the gut. As if she'd been stabbed. As if she were trying to catch her last dying breath.

She was on top of me, her body near perpendicular to mine. Every once in a while she would arch her back. What must have happened is that she'd arched, or tilted, that's more accurate, her head, just enough to glimpse him in a bit of peripheral vision, behind and to the left of where the door to the bedroom was. I was not in a position to see him myself, since every time I tried to lean forward, to thrust my body deeper into hers, she would say, 'No, don't move, don't move!' So I was pretty much just lying there, my pelvis raised, the back of my head flat against the mattress, completely prostrate. I was admiring the headboard, which was made of ash, solid, light ash. She said his name at the same time as she tried to cover herself with the sheets.

'Don't move,' his first words, 'not another muscle.'

She was in the habit of tossing her hands in the air and saying, 'Gil hasn't been home in the middle of the day in forever.' She almost tossed her hands now, but braced herself against the headboard instead. At such a moment, you can tell that someone is not a serial adulterer. Our affair, for her, as I see it, wasn't a natural progression of life. In her age and style of dress, she almost reminded me of my aunt. Or somebody's aunt. On a table near the piano, I once saw a picture of her son.

I must've tried to get up at this point. I remember trying to roll over, or to pull the bed sheet up, but she was still on top of me, and, I think, frozen, unable to move for fear of falling, as if in a car, twisted metal all around her and hanging over the edge of a bridge. Time for both of them must have stopped: no movement, no speech, for fear of what would have to come next. In all the time I'd known her, almost two months, she'd never fallen short for words. Not that she blabbered, just the opposite. Each word she spoke, she spoke for a reason, each word communicated something thought out, something focused. We spent two hours a week together. For half of that time we were on the silent side of sex, beyond the usual, 'O fuck me, just fuck me!' or 'That's it, that's it, I'm going to come.' For the other hour we talked about books. She never spoke about her family, beyond the bit she did to reassure herself that Gil wouldn't come home during the day. She never said, 'Things aren't good.' Never said, 'The bastard has a mistress,' or 'He works too hard.' Instead, she said: 'If the numbers taking vocations get any less, there won't be a Catholic church in fifty years.' Or: 'I'm not sure Wright himself really appreciated the sophistication of the Dana house.' She read two, three books a week, and not your comfortable novels. She liked serious books about literary theory, psychology, archaeology, anthropology; her interests were enormous. I think the last thing we talked about was this biography of Mahler I'd recommended. It explored, in particular, his sessions with Freud after his wife had had an affair. She never said anything about how it affected her personally, of course, but I did think, almost immediately after I recommended it, that the gift of a book detailing the crippling affects of adultery could be seen as insensitive.

'Stay just as you are,' Gil said. 'Just. As. You. Are!'

At first I believed his original instruction was to her, but now that I'm hearing myself say this, pausing like this, I'm wondering if the words were in response to me, my movement, and not to her at all. I was the one trying to get up. In any case, when he spoke, stay I did, still inside her. I was hoping she'd slide off me, but she never did. And my erection never waned. I don't mention this to boast, but to demonstrate the strangeness of the situation – one which was no longer lustful in the least, but one which I couldn't, despite the horror of it, control. Often one sees plays or movies where a man leaps up off the bed and covers himself with a sheet. No signs of an erection poke through.

'Honey,' she said.

'Shut up!' He said. 'Just shut up!'

'But honey!' she said again.

'Honey' is an endearment I've never been partial to. It still strikes me as odd that she used it. I much prefer when couples use the word 'Baby', which, though a bit retro, has, I think, a great ring to it. I think of Tennessee Williams saying to an interviewer, 'You see, baby, after a glass or two of wine I'm inclined to extravagance ... so I'll blue pencil a lot the next day.' She read the book on Williams after I quoted him saying that. I never once called her 'baby', and she never called me 'honey' or 'dear' or 'lovely' or whatever one might call another instead of their name. We weren't inclined to extrava-gance of anything, least of all language. Even with a couple of glasses of wine in me now, I'm telling you this with as little extravagance as I can muster. Our affair was more business than personal. If I had called her 'baby', she probably would have said, 'Please don't call me baby.' And I would have told her how, when I was younger, I once called a girlfriend 'baby', sometimes even 'babe', which I know has a whole different ring to it. I think of real high-end Wall Street sorts, in designer sunglasses and expensive suits, using the word 'babe'. I've worn a suit maybe twice in the past year, for weddings, and I rarely wear sunglasses. Even when it's sunny and sunglasses are practi-cal, I can't bring myself to put them on. I go around the city squinting like an idiot just so I won't look like a guy who calls his girlfriend 'babe'. He, I mean Gil, looked vaguely like one of those guys, but I think I'm only saying this because he was wearing an extremely nice-looking navy pin-striped suit. His hair was dark and closely cropped and parted to the side, only slightly grey around the temples. A good-looking man.

'I want to –' she said.

'Don't!' he said, and he pointed his finger for emphasis.

The bedroom was extremely large. The size of three normal bedrooms at least. I don't know if I've mentioned it, but we were on top of the sheets so he had a full view of us. I think he may have taken a step closer when he said 'Don't!', but I can't be sure. What I am sure about is that when he said 'Don't', his voice fairly boomed. He really shouted it. And then he just sort of trailed off: 'Don't … just don't say anything.' Who can argue with that? I mean what could she say? She stayed hunched over my body while her husband of seventeen years – she once mentioned the year she got married, I did the math – leaned against the wall. You could tell she respected, even loved, this man, because she obliged, even *obeyed*. I take that 'loved' bit back as quickly as I say it; who knows if she loved him or not? All I know is she didn't jump off of me and try to cover herself; she didn't try to force words of explanation, or to run to him; she just kept sitting on top of me, shoulders rounded. She remained uncovered the whole time, her breasts, pert as they still were, jiggling, her back bare, her head tilted just slightly down, her fringe not covering her eyes, her grey-green eyes looking at some place just above my head.

At this point, she must have tried to turn around because he said, 'Don't turn around!' He said, 'Don't look at me, because I can't bear to look at you.'

I'm not sure how the logic of that sentence works exactly, if you untangle it, but I remember it sounding odd, and I think he may have sensed that too because his next words were quick to follow.

'Look at him, just keep looking at him. I can't believe you've done this. Jesus, I can't believe it, I can't fucking believe it! I almost left, you know that? I almost just turned around and left, back down the stairs. You think you have the right to do this? You think you have the right?'

'I don't think I have the –'

'Don't even say that! Jesus Christ!' he said, 'Jesus Fucking Christ.'

At this point he entered the room, and I remember getting nervous. He was pacing a good distance from the bed, ten or so feet, it was a very large bedroom as I've said, and he was almost directly behind her now. I started wondering if he wasn't going to get a baseball bat from the closet and bash our heads in. I wanted to say, 'I should leave,' but I couldn't imagine myself saying anything, so I said nothing. In fact, I never said a word, not once during the entire time. When she finally looked me in the eye, we made the sort of connection that people live their whole lives either wishing or regretting they'd made. I'm thinking of that shared look on passing trains, or in overcrowded clubs, or skiing down a mountain and spotting another watching you from the lift overhead … just before you crash into a tree.

She started talking to him then, while still looking at me. It was odd, let me tell you. I wondered if she knew what she was saying, if she knew just who she was talking to. I wanted to correct the situation, to tell her, 'Your husband is behind you, talk to *him*.' It's difficult to get it right here, but I think I've got the general gist of it down.

'I wish I remembered when we met,' she said. 'I wish I remembered how I once loved you. I wish you still loved me. But you don't. And I don't. So why don't you, just, turn around, and walk back out that door.'

I've said I never spoke to him, which is true, and really, I didn't even think of saying something. But lately, I've been thinking that if I were back in that bed, in that bedroom, I might say, 'Gil' – or maybe not, maybe I wouldn't use his name, maybe just jump right in – 'Listen,' I might've said, 'I don't know you and you don't know me. But you do know your wife.' Wow. I'm glad I didn't say anything.

He moaned, or whimpered. A soft cry. I lifted my head just enough to see him slide down the wall until I couldn't see him anymore. She got off of me and took the bed cover with her – white and silver, dragonflies, and blades of green grass – and wrapped it around herself. I was left naked on the bed, so I began to collect my clothes from the floor and to dress.

'Not another step toward me,' he said, at the bottom of the wall.

She stopped. We were both looking at him. And then he was gone, out the door. She looked at me. She didn't know what to do. And then she ran after him, screaming: 'Gil! Don't leave, Gil!'

But I could hear him rushing down the stairs. I could hear the door slam. I took my time getting dressed, hoping I'd walk into an empty downstairs. I found her in the kitchen; I had to walk through the kitchen to get to the front door. A part of me had imagined her running outside wrapped in the bed cover, her bare legs prickling in the cold wind. Her eyes were red from crying. There was a glass of milk by her arm on the table. A number of books were scattered on the floor. I saw the book on Mahler, the book on Wright, the book on Joyce. She'd been thumbing through a copy of Joyce's letters when I first met her in the bookshop. I walked over to her and said, 'What's amazing about Joyce's letters is that they humanize him. They make him sound like an ordinary man. A normal, jealous man, as insecure as anybody might be when it comes to love.' Those were my first words to her.

She must have swept all the books off the table.

Or *he'd* swept them all off the table.

I don't want to make suppositions about what their life was like before, or after, me, because I don't know. We never talked about the specifics, or even the abstractions, nothing about love or jealousy or about how life is funny or regrettable. But with all of those books on the floor, I wondered if she regretted every word she'd ever read, every word she'd ever taken any pleasure in.

Howling huskies, dangerous trails

ED O'LOUGHLIN

Most people like murder mysteries, or at least they think they do. What they really like is to find out who did it, which is not the same thing at all. A true mystery story, the kind that makes the hairs rise on your neck, should leave you none the wiser, or even less wise than before.

The story of Albert Johnson is one such mystery. It is known, more or less, what he did, eighty years ago this winter, in the Canadian Arctic. What is not known, what is now unknowable, is why he did it. How he did it seems inexplicable, in merely human terms. And who he was remains a riddle.

Adding to the uncanniness of the story is its perfect interplay of character and setting. The drama played itself out in the winter of 1932 in the Northwest and Yukon territories, well above the Arctic Circle, across storm-blasted passes and through forests of stunted spruce and aspen, where the northernmost range of the Rockies meets the frozen Beaufort Sea. For me this is a mythic landscape. As a child, having exchanged the snowy winters of western Canada for the mud and dripping hedges of Country Kildare, I became fascinated with the Arctic and Antarctic, with Greenland sharks and Captain Oates and ice-bound rocks and frozen forests. Near the poles the maps did funny things, projected lines into the void, hinted at eternity; I never much liked globes, which leave less room for mystery.

On a map, the polar regions still appear to be frontiers, though with what it's hard to say exactly; the world is merely round, after all, and the ice is now melting. What struck me about Albert Johnson when I first read about him, sitting up late with whiskey and Wikipedia, was that he was looking for a frontier as he drifted ever-northward. In the end, of course, he found one.

*

Over the past eighty years the Albert Johnson story has spawned at least eight works of popular non-fiction. There have also been two highly fictionalized feature films based on the affair (1981's *Death Hunt* starred Charles Bronson, Lee Marvin and Angie Dickinson), and a recent Discovery Channel documentary. *True Detective* was one of several magazines to publish spreads on the story shortly after it happened, with quotes and testimony from those involved. Yet reliable information on Johnson is hard to come by: the accuracy of the official police report has been drawn into question, and modern authors and journalists have to cope with all the usual distortions of hearsay, sensation, exaggeration, animus, time and forgetfulness, amplified by the remoteness of the region and the tight-lipped instincts of the people who live there.

It is generally accepted, though, that the man known as Albert Johnson first appeared in the Northwest Territories in July 1931, the summer before his death. According to one account, two men of the Gwichin tribe saw a stranger poling a makeshift raft northward on the Peel River, towards the small trading post of Fort McPherson. Because they were expecting the arrival of a stranger from the south, a man named Albert Johnson, they asked the rafter if that was his name. He said that it was.

Some of the clearest information about Johnson comes to us from the traders of Fort McPherson, who were used to weighing up the worth of new arrivals. This one seemed to have plenty of money, and he used it to purchase food, gear, a canoe, a 16-gauge shotgun, and ammunition for the two hunting rifles he already owned, a 30-30 Savage and a .22 Winchester. The managers of both of McPherson's rival fur-trading posts later told the Royal Canadian Mounted Police that Johnson was deliberate in his purchases, quiet to the point of withdrawn, sometimes downright unfriendly. He was in his mid to late thirties, about five foot nine, with light-brown hair and strong legs and shoulders. He spoke with a faint Scandinavian accent.

Rather than stay in the small settlement at Fort McPherson, Johnson camped alone a short way off in the spruce forest, and drove away any Indians who attempted to befriend him. Alerted to his arrival, the senior officer at the nearest RCMP post, Arctic Red River, came to interview the newcomer; in Canada, unlike the US, the frontier police had a welfare role, and would send back to the south any new arrival whom they thought would not survive the winter. The wilds of Alaska and northern Canada had long attracted loners, adventurers and frontiersmen, who prospected for gold and silver in the short summers and spent the winters trapping fox and marten for their furs. They called themselves 'sourdoughs' after their practice of carrying a ball of sourdough in a pouch round their neck; the warm dough was used as a starter to leaven bread, in an environment where yeast would not survive long. At times, however, these skilled survivors were joined by large numbers of ill-prepared 'cheechakos' (a Chinook word meaning newcomer). In 1896 the Klondike gold strike had brought a hundred thousand stampeders to the Yukon territory, including a few score who managed to pass the longest, hardest route of all, floating down the Mackenzie River to Fort McPherson, then dragging their boats up the shallow, rapids-strewn Rat River and over the continental watershed to Loon Lake. In 1931, when Johnson arrived, the Great Depression was driving many desperate men northward.

Approached in a Fort McPherson store, Johnson reluctantly told Constable Edgar Millen that he intended to pass the winter trapping for furs along the Rat River, and that he had spent the previous year in the prairies. Millen suspected this to be untrue: he had already heard that Johnson had come down the Peel River, which rose on the border of the Yukon to the west, and not down the Mackenzie, which was the only practical direct route from the prairies, a thousand miles to the south. But the prospectors and fur trappers who wandered the north were fond of covering their tracks, often for good commercial reasons, so the policeman merely advised Johnson that he would have to obtain a trapping licence from the regional RCMP headquarters in Aklavik, sixty miles further down the Peel where it joins the Mackenzie Delta.

Johnson next came to the attention of the authorities on Boxing Day, when a small party of Indians came to Millen's post at Arctic Red River to complain that the white man, who had built a winter cabin more than a day's travel north of McPherson on the Rat River, had been interfering with their fur traps. Having learned by radio that Johnson still had no trapping permit, Millen sent a two-man patrol to have another word with him. It was an overnight trip for the two Mounties, travelling with dog sleds through deep snow, but the following day, when Constable Alfred King knocked on the cabin door, Johnson merely peered out the window then closed the curtain. This was very odd behaviour for the northlands, where hospitality to travellers was a firm custom. After a fruitless hour of knocking and calling, the policemen decided to mush eighty miles onward to Aklavik, to obtain a search warrant from their regional commander.

Four days later, on New Year's Eve 1931, Constable King again knocked at Johnson's cabin, warrant in hand, with three other officers standing by to support him, and was shot through the chest by a 30-30 bullet, fired through the door.

It was blowing a blizzard, the fine dust-like snow of the Mackenzie Delta drifting waist-deep over the frozen rivers and rough portages. Fortunately for King, command of the four-man expedition now devolved to Constable R.G. McDowell, a champion dog-sledder. With McDowell setting the pace, they travelled through the night, covering the eighty miles in a remarkable twenty hours. The three uninjured men had to break trail with their snowshoes through the deep, fresh snow all the way back, stumbling and falling, the sweat freezing in their clothes, to make a path for the sled which bore King. They reached the hospital in Aklavik just in time to save King's life.

King recovered well enough to be wounded again in the Second World War, serving with an RCMP detachment in Italy. Later, looking back on his life, he said of Johnson, 'All I wanted to tell him was to leave the Indians' traps alone. Then all he had to do was get a trapper's licence and he was all set.'

Instead, Johnson was now an attempted cop-killer. The regional RCMP commander in Aklavik, Inspector Alexander Eames, called for civilian volunteers, and summoned his handful of available constables and special constables – native Americans and 'half-breeds', hired locally to support the white officers from the south. When his eleven-strong posse reached the Rat River cabin on 9 January, they were astounded to see that its chimney was smoking. Johnson was waiting for them.

The eight-by-ten-foot cabin was stoutly built of spruce logs dug into a pit in the ground: it offered Johnson both shelter and cover. He had made loopholes in the walls which allowed him to cover all the approaches to the cabin; the barrels and stocks of his shotgun and .22 had been sawn off to create makeshift handguns. Thus armed and fortified, Johnson held off the posse in a sixteen-hour gun battle. The besiegers threw dynamite to try to blast him out, but it was rendered almost useless by the extreme cold; while Johnson sat tight, his enemies froze.

Early next morning, with food running short, Eames and his posse retreated to Aklavik. When they were gone, the trapper slipped off into the forest. The weapons and gear that he carried were later found to have weighed almost as much as he did; they can still be inspected today at the RCMP's museum in Regina, Saskatchewan. For transport, Johnson had only his homemade snowshoes, woven to his own unique pattern. Yet such was his stamina that when Eames and his men returned to the hunt their trackers calculated that Johnson was averaging two miles on foot for every mile they managed with their dogs, travelling in long zig-zags so he could secretly observe his pursuers, often circling back behind them. To spare his energy and minimize his tracks, he favoured the wind-hardened snow along ridges, and would cross creeks only on featureless ice. At one point, two trackers who were separately following fragments of his trail came face to face; he had, they realized, stopped at that point to put his snowshoes on backward.

Instead of fleeing directly west – he might have made it to lawless Alaska

– Johnson seemed to be playing games with his pursuers. Perhaps he underestimated the Mounties' famous doggedness, and hoped they would abandon the hunt. He might have been trying to circle back to food caches hidden near his cabin – caches that, unbeknownst to him, the Mounties were watching. But with so many patrols now fanned out across his trail – thirty men were involved at the height of the hunt – he was never able to circle quite far enough out to slip back behind them.

On 30 January, a month after King's shooting, a four-man patrol led by Edgar Millen came across Johnson as he made camp in a thicket on a creek off the Rat River. Although they could not see him, they heard him cough and move in the trees.

Hearing their approach, Johnson dived into cover. Both sides opened fire. Eventually the shooting stopped, and the posse lay silent in the snow for two more hours, thinking that Johnson was hit but afraid to go nearer. Finally Millen – thirty-one years old, Belfast-born, the best step-dancer and pastry cook in the western Arctic and the only policeman to speak to Johnson face to face – lost patience in the extreme cold. He charged Johnson's position and was immediately shot dead. The rest of the posse withdrew.

The trapper had now wounded one policeman and killed another and the authorities seemed no closer to catching him. The manhunt was grabbing headlines across the world; one early dispatch referred to Johnson as 'the mad trapper of Rat River', a name that has stuck ever since. According to Dick North, author of several books on the incident, the manhunt became such a sensation that it was hard to hail a cab in New York City when a radio bulletin was due. At the height of the Great Depression, many ordinary people sympathized with Johnson, taking him for a poor drifter hounded by the law.

In desperation, Eames took the unprecedented step of requesting that a search plane be sent up from the south. He later wrote in his official account of the manhunt: 'I note in the press reports that Johnson is referred to as "the demented trapper". On the contrary, he showed himself to be an extremely shrewd and resolute man, capable of quick thought and action. A tough and desperate character.' The pilot selected for the search mission was himself already a legend in Canada. On his first combat patrol over France in 1918, Lieutenant Wilfrid 'Wop' May had nearly become the eighty-first victim of Baron Manfred Von Richthofen, the First World War's most famous fighter ace; instead, the 'Red Baron' was himself shot down and killed, either by ground fire or by another Canadian pilot, and May survived to become an ace himself. After the war, he pioneered the Arctic airmail run, and made global headlines by rushing diphtheria vaccine to a stricken northern outpost.

It took May four storm-battered days to fly the thousand miles to the Arctic from his base at Fort McMurray, Alberta, but once it joined the search his Bellanca monoplane proved invaluable. Trails that would baffle ground parties for days could be scouted in minutes from the air. Army signallers stationed at Aklavik improvised a sled-mounted two-way radio, so that for the first time the searchers could communicate in real time with the aircraft and their base.

This technological escalation forced Johnson to change his tactics. He could no longer be under any illusion that time was on his side; worse, he was starving. For a month he had been walking up to thirty miles a day in deep snow and broken country, crawling through thickets, humping well over a hundred pounds of gear. Scientists later estimated that he was burning about ten thousand calories a day – the equivalent of two marathon runs. His Indian trackers knew from studying his camps that he was using smokeless willow twigs to light small fires in caves dug from drifts, boiling up snow to make drinking water. Unable to shoot game because of the need for stealth and silence, he was reduced to snaring animals and birds. The trackers now began to see the first signs of unsteadiness in his gait, as hunger and exhaustion weakened him.

When a blizzard swept down from the north, grounding the plane for three days, Johnson took advantage of the respite to slog across the

Richardson Mountains into the Yukon. Alone, on foot and without climbing gear, he scaled a seven-thousand-foot peak in the blizzard. In three days he travelled ninety miles on foot, battling deep snow, storm-force winds and a temperature of minus 45 degrees centigrade. At least one night was spent in the high mountain passes, without shelter or firewood. It seemed an almost supernatural achievement: local Gwichin trackers, specialist mountain survivors, had told the RCMP that it could not be done; they could not have done it themselves.

It was the same radio broadcasts that had stirred sympathy for Johnson that finally did for him. Near La Pierre House, a trading post in the northern Yukon, some trappers heard a bulletin from Alaska, and thought of the strange tracks they had noticed close by. The news was rushed by dog-sled back across the Continental Divide. Hitching a lift in May's aircraft, it took Eames and his advance party a mere forty minutes to cross the barren passes and deep snow that had taxed Johnson's strength for days.

Five days later the man known as Albert Johnson came face-to-face with Staff Sergeant Earl Hersey on a frozen bend of the Eagle River. They opened fire on each other, and Hersey – an army signaller and former Olympic runner – fell, seriously injured. But the rest of the posse closed in on the trapper, firing from the high banks on either side of the river, just as May's plane appeared overhead. One bullet struck a box of .22 rounds in Johnson's back pocket, blowing his hip apart. Ignoring calls for his surrender, he took cover behind his heavy pack, clawed a shallow hole in the snow and calmly returned fire. Several more shots struck him before his rifle fell silent. May, swooping low overhead, saw the stillness of his posture and waggled his wings to signal the end. He then landed on the ice to evacuate Hersey.

The only food the Mounties found on Johnson was a frozen squirrel and a jay. He was severely emaciated, his face and limbs black from frostbite, yet his tracks showed that only minutes earlier he had found the strength to climb a tree to spy out the land. Later, hidden under the butt-plate of his 30-

30 rifle, the police found a hand-carved compartment containing a single bullet. Johnson had decided, probably a long time before, that he would not be taken alive.

The authorities performed an autopsy and sent photographs and fingerprints to law-enforcement agencies across Canada and the Unites States. It was assumed that Johnson would prove to be a notorious felon, with reason to fight to the death, but no matching photos or fingerprints have ever been found. Johnson may or may not have thought that he was wanted, but it seems that he was not.

Rumours and theories abounded. Johnson's skill in battle persuaded many that he was a haunted veteran of the Great War. To others, his sawn-off weapons suggested a professional criminal, with a history of gangsterism. John Evans, a director of the Canadian Police Research Center in Edmonton who has researched the affair, mentioned this point in the course of a phone interview with me. 'You need barrel length for accuracy, so sawing your weapons down makes them no good for hunting,' he said. 'It's more for close-in work – so you can conceal the weapon. He might have wanted a handgun, but people up there don't have a lot of use for handguns.'

In 1932, despite strong opposition from the local community, the Mounties buried Johnson in Aklavik's public cemetery. In 2009 a team of scientists sponsored by the Discovery Channel obtained permission to exhume the corpse to perform modern forensic tests. Over the decades, a number of people across North America and Scandinavia had plausibly claimed that the 'Mad Trapper' might have been their long-lost relative. But as Barbara Smith recounts in her book on the exhumation, DNA tests disproved every claim.

The most interesting results came from a study of the dead man's teeth. According to Dr David Sweet, a forensic odontologist at the University of British Columbia, Johnson had in his adult life obtained expensive and innovative dental surgery, including gold bridgework and white fillings. Such advanced dentistry would at that time have been available only to wealthy people, in only a handful of cities in the US. Johnson had not been a poor drifter all his life.

The mystery of Albert Johnson has many facets, and one of them is literary: how do we know that our narrators are telling us the truth? Much of what we think we know about the whole affair comes from the official report on the manhunt written by Inspector Eames. But Barbara Smith has uncovered a fragment of another contemporary police report which questions the credibility of Eames's account. This second account was written by Constable William Carter, who was sent by the RCMP commanders in Edmonton to join the manhunt and to secretly spy on Eames's performance.

Having reinterviewed many of the principals, Carter concluded that 'the expenditure of ammunition by Johnson was minimal compared to [what was written in] the official report' and that Eames's document, 'intended as it was for official and public consumption, is lax in detailing some of the incidents, and covers up many blunders'. Sadly, only a fragment of Carter's report has survived, and so what those blunders might have been, like so much else, is unclear. But Carter came to a somewhat different reading of the fugitive whom Eames judged 'extremely shrewd and resolute ... tough and desperate'. 'Why,' Carter wrote, 'did he hang around the country after each confrontation? My explanation which seems to me logical as any, is that the man was bushed [maddened by darkness and isolation] and retaliated like any hunted animal by running away and fighting only when cornered.'

Today Aklavik is a sprawl of wooden houses and outbuildings set on a low ridge above the Peel River, home to six hundred people, mostly Gwichin or Inuvialuit 'Eskimos'. On a clear day, the Richardson mountains can be seen to the west. The name means 'place of the barren land grizzlies', referring to the barren tundra of the high Arctic, which begins at the treeline, only a few miles to the north. The town can be reached by car only in winter, when ice-roads are ploughed into the Peel and Mackenzie rivers.

Johnson's grave, unlike the others in the cemetery, is confined by a white picket fence. When I visited Aklavik last February, as part of a trip to research a book, I had to dig down through three feet of snow to uncover the small white wooden cross. On it was printed: 'Albert Johnson?'

Across the road stood a wooden cut-out of a man in a parka and snow-boots holding a rifle. There was a hole where the face should have been, so that the few tourists who come this way can have a novelty photograph of themselves posing as the Mad Trapper. Nearby was a sign with this inscription:

> Albert Johnson arrived in Ross River August 21 1927. Complaints of local trapper brought the RCMP on him. He shot two officers and became a fugitive of the law with howling huskies, dangerous trails, frozen nights. The posse finally caught up with him. He was killed up the Eagle River Feb 17, 1932.

The date of 1927 and the reference to Ross River – a trading post in the Yukon about four hundred miles south of Fort McPherson – arise from research conducted by police and later by Dick North which strongly suggests that Albert Johnson was previously known in the Yukon as Arthur Nelson, a prospector and trapper. Nelson too was an inscrutable loner, and some who met him found him frightening. But Nelson had no known history of violence, and on occasion demonstrated kindness and generosity. What drove the man we know as Albert Johnson ever further northward, outward, into himself, can only be guessed at. Such journeys were not uncommon in the northlands, and some still make them now. He may have thought that the Northwest Territories would be a further step into silence. He may not have foreseen the policemen, and the permits, and the radios.

*

Several years ago, after decades of legwork, Dick North managed to identify Arthur Nelson – the man he believes is Albert Johnson – in the corner of a photograph taken at the Ross River trading post in 1930: he appears blond, shy of the camera; perhaps he is half-smiling. For me, this grainy print has a crypto-zoological fascination, like a photo of Sasquatch, or a ghostly blur in the background of a holiday snap.

During the manhunt, many trappers and Indians abandoned their isolated cabins and took their families to Aklavik and Fort McPherson and Arctic Red River, seeking refuge from the killer who wandered in the snow. For some, Johnson became associated with the legendary Bushman, a spirit that lives in the forests and wastes. Peter Esau, an eighty-year-old native of Aklavik and himself a former special constable, told me how as a little boy his mother would tell him to be good, 'or Albert Johnson will get you'.

John Steinbeck wrote that 'An ocean without its unnamed monsters would be like a completely dreamless sleep'. Standing in the frozen forest, it is easy to call Johnson, like Bigfoot, from the trees.

Ireland on fire

RACHEL ANDREWS

1

In early May of last year, when gorse and forest fires began burning across Co. Donegal, Tony Finnerty took a call from a forest caretaker near Dungloe, on the county's Atlantic coast. It was a Saturday, almost ten at night. Finnerty is a manager with Coillte, the state-owned forest management company. He is also an accomplished amateur musician, and he was tired from a late session the previous night at the Cup of Tae traditional music festival, which takes place annually in the small town of Ardara. He spoke to the caretaker for a while, and began making his own phone calls. 'I arranged for a team of people, people who have helped me in the past, to go out and be available to the fire officer,' he told me when I met him two months later.

Finnerty had the numbers of forty-five such people in his mobile phone. These were neighbours, friends, local farmers. Because the fire began at a weekend, and because 'when you call men there's some at weddings, there are some at funerals, there are some in bed, there are some sick, there are some have a few drinks, there are some at parties', it took him a while to put together a team of fifteen, including himself. He ate a sandwich and drank a cup of tea, then left his house in Portnoo, about eight miles south-west of Dungloe as the crow flies but twice that on the winding coastal roads, for the Dungloe area, where together with his team and a fire officer he assessed the potential danger of a substantial fire that was moving westwards across gorse and bogland and threatening Glenveagh National Park, the villages of Doochary, Lettermacaward and Dungloe, and a hundred-acre block of Coillte forest.

'I felt that there was time,' Finnerty, who is brisk and garrulous, told me. 'It was travelling on open ground and I felt that at the rate it was burning there would be time to go out in the morning at first light and put out the fire.' The team agreed to meet at first light, and Finnerty went home. It was 4 a.m. He slept until 5.15, then got up and went out again. For three hours he and his men, armed with fire-beating shovels known as flappers – a broad piece of rubber mounted on a handle – attempted to keep the fire from reaching the forest. They fanned out in groups of five along the fire line, with three members of each group standing at the face of the fire, and the other two behind tramping out any sparks that might have reignited, rotating their positions as the heat became too much for those at the front. The flames were large and intense, but by half past eight on Sunday morning Finnerty and his men had shortened the length of the fire front by about a mile and a half and he was hopeful of saving the forest.

2

In a country as wet as Ireland, it seems inconceivable that wildfire should pose a serious problem. Yet in the past ten years the frequency of wild gorse and forest fires in this country has been increasing steadily; there are now around four thousand wildfires per year. Most of these are started intentionally by farmers trying to control the growth of scrub on their grazing land, but get out of control and run wild. The past two years have seen wildfire damage on an unprecedented scale. In 2010 Coillte reported the loss of over 1,900 acres of forestry from wildfire, and last May the company lost 2,400 acres: during the same period as the fires in Donegal, there were also serious fires in Mayo, Galway, Meath, Westmeath, Offaly, Louth and Monaghan. The damage caused by wildfire is not, of course, confined to forestry: brush fires can be very destructive, and place a heavy firefighting and financial burden on local authorities. 'It is vital we don't have a repeat of the record numbers of fires last year,' said Adrian Kelly, Clare's chief fire officer and vice chairman of the Irish Chief Fire Officers' Association, in a statement published on 29 April 2011. The fires in Donegal began the next day.

There are a number of reasons behind the recent spike in wildfires. The unusually cold winters of the past few years have killed off vegetation that would normally survive the winter, leaving it ready to ignite when the weather becomes warmer. (It remains to be seen whether the milder winter of 2011–12 will be followed by a quieter fire season.) Arson, too, could be a factor: Gardaí investigated claims that the fires in Donegal were started maliciously by young people throwing firelighters from cars, and Tony Finnerty theorized about those who 'would deliberately burn our forests', either because of a historical view of forestry as an activity that chased farmers off the land, or out of a more general anger towards the state. 'There are a lot of people cross out there for loads of reasons,' he said. 'There are different people who are at different levels of frustration, and they have different ways of releasing it.'

But a more fundamental, and more complex, cause of the increase in wildfire is the changing use – and hence the changing ecology – of Irish scrubland. For centuries, Irish farmers have deliberately burned gorse, bracken, hazel and other scrub, as well as the less palatable grasses, such as older heather and purple moor grass, to stop the spread of undesirable vegetation and to stimulate regrowth for grazing. Burning kills the top growth on plants, and sheep are attracted to the young shoots on newly burnt heather and the fresh grass that grows alongside the re-sprouting heather plants.

Farmers habitually burn their lands in the springtime, usually between March and May, when there are dry periods but also sufficient moisture to protect roots and soil from damage. Until 2000, they were legally allowed to burn scrubland between 31 August and 14 April. Since then – due to an amendment to the Wildlife Act intended to protect nesting and breeding birds and other wildlife – it has been illegal to burn after 1 March. Farmers are now regularly warned by the authorities that they could be fined, imprisoned, or risk losing their EU Single Farm Payment if they burn illegally. A Land and Forest Fires Working Group, set up by the Department of Agriculture, recommended in January 2011 that farmers be properly trained in control burning and made aware of the consequences of acting outside the current legislation. Despite the Working Group's recognition that the burning of land is an accepted farm-management practice, and despite a series of separate information pamphlets issued by the Department, which also attempt to take account of farmers' wish to burn, the issue remains one of conflict: between a law that tells farmers they cannot burn when they want to burn and farmers who say the law stops them from burning when they must burn.

Late last summer, in the midst of a day-long downpour, I drove to Killarney to meet Ciaran Nugent, a Forestry Inspector with the Department of Agriculture, Food and Marine. Nugent, who is tall and rangy and speaks with a trace of a Dublin accent, had recently circulated a forty-page Draft Code of Practice for Prescribed Burning among farming and environmental organizations, with the intention of developing a final code that would act as a guide for farmers and other landowners. There are several hundred wildfires in Kerry in an average year. In April 2010 a gorse fire caused widespread destruction of young deer and nesting birds and came within two metres of a major forest in Killarney National Park; later in the same week a gorse fire that broke out at Glenfisk, near Killarney, threatened four homes and burned for over seven hours. Nugent, whose remit is to protect and develop forests, had in the past found himself in the unwelcome position of prosecuting landowners for illegal burning. He was more interested in finding solutions to the problem, and since 2003 he had been making earnest efforts to engage with the local farming community; when we met, he was able to speak with authority on matters such as grazing rights and regimes, depopulation and stocking levels.

'I view fire as being primarily a social issue, although we have these other physical, geographic elements to it,' Nugent said. 'The issue with fire is about humans, it's about human interaction with the landscape.'

He talked about the ways in which Irish people have transformed their interaction with the landscape, particularly over the past ten years. 'There's a new type of people living in rural areas that don't manage land, they're not farming, they're living a suburban lifestyle effectively. We've a lot of one-off housing in some of these rural areas so there are people in proximity to fire incidents that wouldn't have been there previously.' The expansion of forestry, too, means that in places like Kerry forestry plantations are 'cheek-by-jowl with these areas that are subject to fire risk' to a greater degree than ever before.

Meanwhile, the farmers are fewer and more elderly, and on the upland farms of the Atlantic seaboard they are keeping their animals on ever larger areas of commonage – land on which two or more farmers have grazing rights – that tends to be less well managed than in the past. Changes in the numbers and types of livestock on the mountains and hillsides have also played a part. While farmers traditionally kept a mix of cattle and sheep on their upland farms, for many years EU policies and subsidies favoured sheep production, which led to a growing population of sheep and a declining population of cattle. The cows had been hardy local types, and farmers could depend on them to deal with the awkward vegetation – gorse and hard rush and bracken – that sheep find too rough but that cattle will either graze on or trample down. The rapid increase in sheep numbers – the total number of sheep in Ireland almost tripled after the inclusion of sheep meat within the Single Market in 1980 – also affected the ecology of the uplands: because sheep will congregate in areas of better forage, severe overgrazing did terrible damage to heather and bare peat, and encouraged the dominance of poorer grasses and sedge species.

In the late 1990s the government attempted to address this by instituting a compulsory sheep cull of 30 per cent on all commonages. Farmers now blame this measure – along with the Rural Environment Protection Scheme (REPS), which encouraged farmers to reduce stocking levels – for the subsequent problem of too few sheep, resulting in undergrazing and a surge in the density of scrub in upland areas, which they say has left them with no option but to control-burn larger areas than in the past – sometimes entire hillsides – and with greater frequency. In May 2011, nineteen Irish environmental NGOs prepared a briefing note for the European Commission that cited another cause of increased use of fire by farmers: a new EU provision whereby scrubland is not counted towards 'eligible hectares' for subsidy under the Single Payments Scheme.

Now farmers feel as though they are on the back foot. At a consultation forum late last August in Killarney, seven local farmers discussed the problem of wildfires with Matt Carroll, a professor at the Department of Natural Resource Sciences at Washington State University, who was undertaking research on the subject. Most of the farmers were in their fifties or sixties, and they had the weather-hardened look of men who spend their days in the open air. The oldest and most charismatic among them was Ted Horan, an Irish Farmers' Association official, whose wrist and finger were strapped in a white bandage. As Horan made his points he occasionally banged his hand on the table.

He told Carroll that the changes to the burning dates had 'made criminals out of us that were doing it properly'. Since the changes, farmers had three options: to burn illegally, on their own land or commonage, and take the risk of being caught; to burn illegally on commonage and to run from the fire, ensuring no control and making it almost impossible for the authorities to assign responsibility ('the fire service when they go to a fire, they're supposed to find who started the fire, but they never seem to find them,' said Horan); or to allow their lands to become overgrown. The farmers talked about the difficulty of trying to burn within the legal timeframe – in a 2009 survey of farming in Kerry's Iveragh uplands, over 40 per cent of farmers said they felt it was impossible to burn in the legal period due to wet weather – and said that most commonage mountains in south Kerry are now at risk of serious wildfire because of a lack of controlled burning.

'The mountains were always managed by burning,' said Ted Horan. 'The burning of the mountain for the traditional mountain farmer was as important as setting the potatoes, setting the oats; that was an important job, he went out and he did it, if he was able to do it on his own he did it, he got help with him if 'twas needed.' When the day for burning came – traditionally at some point during late March or the first few weeks in April – farmers would assess the position of the wind and would burn their land in strips of about ten feet, controlling the fire with fire breaks and frequently with help from neighbours. The changes to the burning dates, as well as the decline in population among hill-farming communities – the Iveragh uplands survey also found that 50 per cent of farmers no longer burn because of a lack of manpower and a fear that the fires might get out of control – have impacted on these traditions. Farmers are concerned that knowledge of how to manage a fire, traditionally handed down to children as they accompanied their parents on a burn, is in danger of being lost.

If it is lost, there will likely be more incidents of poorly executed burning, as farmers burn on their own, or against the wind, or in conditions that are too hot or too windy. In February 2010 an elderly farmer was killed while burning gorse and withered grass on his land in Killarney, but more often the consequences involve damage to the land. A well-orchestrated burn will create a fast fire that moves quickly across vegetation and burns off the old growth, but if the fire is hot and slow it will heat the soil and sterilize the new shoots of heather and other vegetation farmers are trying to encourage for grazing. This sort of burning can also lead to soil erosion, and it can take many years for the ground to recover.

3

By the third week of April last year, Met Éireann confirmed that all the conditions that facilitate the rapid spread of wildfires were evident: it was dry and warm (in most places temperatures were around three degrees higher than normal), it was windy, and rainfall was well below average. On 19 April the Department of Agriculture issued a long press release aimed primarily at landowners and farmers. 'Last year, thousands of acres of valuable forestry was [sic] lost due to illegal and careless land burning, while the extent of the destruction of wildlife and natural habitats remains incalculable,' it stated. 'Please DO NOT LIGHT FIRES IN OR NEAR WOODLAND.'

The Donegal fires started on the afternoon of Saturday, 30 April – the last day of the warmest April on record in Ireland. The temperature was 20 degrees and a strong wind was blowing from the east. It was a bank holiday weekend, and local news websites carried stories predicting a record number of Easter visitors to the Donegal beaches. All that day, into the evening, and over the following few days, 120 members of the fire service – almost the entire Donegal force – were despatched to separate blazes across the county. There were fires off the main road between Ardara and Glenties; at Portnoo; at Ballyshannon, near Bundoran; on the Inishowen and Fanad peninsulas at the northern tip of the county; and on Muckish, a distinctive flat-topped mountain in the Derryveagh range, where a lot of damage was done to wildlife. According to Birdwatch Ireland, thousands of birds in the middle of the nesting season, including stonechats, whitethroats, linnets, blackbirds, dunnocks and meadow pipits, were killed, as well as millions of insects and other sources of food. The cuckoo, a protected species, also suffered, because it nests in other birds' nests. The number and extent of the fires strained resources and exhausted firefighters, who told journalists the fires were the worst in living memory.

On Sunday, the Army and Air Corps were called in to help. Over four days, more than 150 members of the Defence Forces, wearing specialist fire-fighting suits, along with three Air Corps helicopters and three Coillte helicopters, were deployed in the area, and there was dramatic television footage of thousands of litres of water being dropped from the air. No one was killed, but the fire around Ballyshannon destroyed the wooden house of Ursula Stein, a woman in her eighties who was taken in by neighbours before the flames reached her, and in Ardara, according to witnesses, thirty-foot flames licked the homes of evacuated residents. Along the route between Dungloe and Doochary, where the worst of the Donegal fires raged until Wednesday morning, householders were also asked to evacuate. Some elderly farmers lost the stashes of turf that they had built up and kept close to their homes for use in the years when they would not be able to get to the bog. Crops were destroyed, along with hundreds of kilometres of fencing and other farm infrastructure. For over a fortnight after the fires were contained, until 19 May, the bogs continued to smoulder.

Tony Finnerty understands fire. He was brought up in the country, his father a forester before him, steeped in nature, history, geography. He understands the wildlife and geology, the wind and weather, and the farming practices in his part of Ireland. He can name at a glance the different grasses that grow on the bogs and hillsides of west Donegal and he knows how those grasses behave in a fire: for example, the purple moor grass that the farmers call the *fionnán* turns into tinder when it dries out in the frost. He'll explain to you that in a woodland, it's not the trees that initially catch fire but the vegetation in the understorey, and that, of the tree species that predominate in Irish forests, the spruce casts a particularly dense shade and stunts the growth of ground vegetation, meaning there is less chance of a fire starting in a spruce plantation; in pine forest, by contrast, the trees let in more light, and a fire will travel through the grasses and other combustible vegetation on the ground. He told me that the infertile peat soil in which most of the Coillte forests are planted kept burning after the other flames were put out, and caused trees and grasses to re-ignite.

The fire threatening the Coillte forest near Dungloe, which Finnerty believed he and his team had brought under control, started advancing again later on the Sunday morning, fuelled by the east wind. When that happened, he took his men to a nearby river that flowed between the fire and the forest, and worked at containing the fire along a line within five hundred metres of the wood. To control it they needed to start back-burning: starting a controlled fire in vegetation that lay in the path of the wildfire, thereby depriving it of fuel. In order to contain the controlled fire, Finnerty needed to wet a road that lay between the forest and the river. From there, he planned to burn back to the river. Finnerty's difficulty was that he had no access to water, and none of the men working with him had a pump that they could have used in the river. There were fire brigades stationed up the road with full tanks of water, but they were tasked with defending houses and told him they couldn't risk losing their supply, even though the green ground surrounding those houses would almost certainly be enough to protect them: along roads affected by the fires, flames swallowed up trees and scrubland no more than fifteen or twenty feet away from residential properties, while the houses stood untouched in their lawns. But the fire service has a hierarchy of priorities: lives first, then homes. Forestry is further down the list. Without water, Finnerty could not save his wood, and the forest at Dungloe was burned from end to end on the Sunday evening.

Tony Finnerty fought various fires in the Donegal forests from first thing Sunday morning until the early hours of Wednesday, when they were finally put out, having burned thousands of acres of Coillte woods around Dungloe, and at Doochary and Glenties. For much of the time he was firefighting, Finnerty was working close to his house, which gardaí urged him to evacuate on the Monday evening. 'The services came up and down the road with loudspeakers,' he said. Finnerty's daughter, a school principal who lives nearby, chose to evacuate her own house, taking her filing cabinet with her. But

Finnerty and his wife decided to stay. The fire shot sparks onto a pile of timber Finnerty had by the side of the house, and flames carried on the wind scorched tall trees growing to the front. His wife, at home making dinner, was nervous, fearful the house might go up. Some local men had come earlier with their slurry tankers and sprayed the trees with water. Later, when he watched a home video his daughter had made from a rocky vantage point down the hillside from his house, Finnerty wondered how the house had escaped. On the day I met him, he drove me to that vantage point, and we looked up the hill to his house. 'I couldn't envisage it,' he said, 'but they were actually licking the house, they were licking the house, the flames.'

4

Though it can be difficult to imagine when looking at today's Irish landscape of bare hills, cultivated fields and grazed pastures, the country was once covered in a blanket of woodland. In his book *Forestry in Ireland*, Niall O'Carroll quotes the medieval clergyman Giraldus Cambrensis, who noted at the end of the twelfth century that 'Ireland is well-wooded and marshy. The plains are of limited extent compared with the woods.' By the beginning of the twentieth century, a range of factors – the plantations of Ireland (during which landlords cleared large areas of forest cover to create agricultural land), intense population growth in the eighteenth and early nineteenth centuries, and advancements in farming – had destroyed around 80 per cent of Ireland's forests. The deforestation of Ireland over this period was more dramatic than that in any other European country.

The Land Acts of the late nineteenth and early twentieth centuries, which provided for the transfer of land from landlords to tenant farmers, encouraged farmers to clear the land for tillage and grazing, and landlords about to lose their estates often cashed in their timber crops in advance. In 1919, the state-run Forestry Commission was established, with the remit of acquiring and managing land for forestry purposes, and this body was retained after independence. But it wasn't until the introduction of the Forestry Act in 1946 that the government brought in a yearly planting quota; by 1948 an annual afforestation target of 25,000 acres had been agreed, along with a plan to plant a million acres within forty years. The latter goal was eventually achieved – between state and private planting – in 1991. Private planting had begun in earnest during the late 1980s, with the introduction of EU grants to encourage farmers and non-farming individuals or companies to undertake forestry, primarily for the commercial production of timber. By the early 1990s there were plantations in all twenty-six counties, with the largest amount of private planting taking place in Cork, Kerry, Clare, Galway, Mayo and Donegal. Foresters had been directed to aim for a mix of species, but the poor land allocated for planting meant two kinds of tree predominated: the Sitka spruce and the Lodgepole pine, neither of which is native to Ireland. (The forests damaged in Donegal mostly comprised these tree types.)

The forest policy of independent Ireland for much of the twentieth century was informed in part by 'land hunger'. Memories of tenant farmers struggling to survive on inferior land, and the resulting intense attachment to the idea of Ireland as a society dominated by communities of small farms, led to successive governments allowing forestry to be planted only on the poorest and most unproductive soil. Officially, this policy has changed to promote more diverse planting on richer lands; in practice the emphasis remains on conifers planted in soil unfavourable to agriculture.

In 1989, the Forestry Commission was re-launched as Coillte. Today, the state-owned company owns over one million acres of land, but as private tree planting has expanded it has scaled back its own afforestation programme, and increasingly works with farmers – who make up around 80 per cent of private planters – who want to become involved in forestry. Changes to the structure and staffing levels of the organization, and an increased dependence on private contractors, have affected its ability to protect its own plantations. Some landowners remember a time when Coillte operated a fire patrol around forest areas from mid February to mid May; those working on the patrols travelled by bicycle – or occasionally motorbike – and carried a flapper to quench fires shortly after they started. Although it is generally accepted that the state's forestry sector was once overstaffed, redundancies and cutbacks have left less staff available to work locally on fire prevention and mitigation, and the controlled preventive burning of forest undergrowth is happening less frequently than in the past. Adrian Kelly, the Clare fire chief, told me that there are similar problems in private forestry, as forest owners seek to reduce costs by cutting back on understorey management.

For those who subscribe to the notion that some of the recent wildfires were started deliberately, there is one overriding explanation: some Irish people don't like forests. Certainly, there is a history of resentment towards forestry in this country. In his book *Bad Blood*, an account of a walk along the Irish border from Derry to Newry during the summer after the Anglo-Irish agreement, Colm Tóibín describes arriving in recession-devastated Leitrim. 'Trees had become a deeply emotional issue in Leitrim,' he wrote, 'as private investors became involved in buying up land for forestry. Farmers whose families had tilled a thirty-acre plot for generations were dismayed to find that their neighbours had sold up and the farm beside them was to become a forest.'

In 2006, research among communities in counties Roscommon, Leitrim, Sligo and Cavan found that local landowners viewed forestry – with the EU subsidies it attracts – as a source of competition for land they expected to be able to buy in order to consolidate their small holdings, while the purchase of land by private institutions – investment companies or individuals, often based in Dublin – fuelled allusions to absentee landlordism. People didn't like the tree species planted – the non-native pines and spruces – which they felt interfered with the landscape, and they didn't like how mature trees blocked views and isolated neighbours. According to the study, the opposition reached a peak in 1987 when machinery that was being used in afforestation within the case-study area was damaged. The research also found that trees were seen as a kind of depopulating agent: people were being replaced by forests.

Tóibín described this feeling in his book. 'I walked along through the boggy terrain where a few scrawny-looking haystacks lay in the fields, through the landscape dotted with abandoned houses, and stretches of new forests. There was no sense of habitation anywhere, the population having decreased from 150,000 to 27,000 between 1841 and 1986 because of emigration, famine and now forestry.'

The past few decades have seen something of a softening in public attitudes towards the industry, as the expansion of financial incentives for ordinary farmers to grow trees as crops has given them grounds to consider forestry as a viable option that is not antithetical to farming. Currently, around 11 per cent of the country is covered in forest, which is still an extremely low percentage in comparison to other European countries. Government policy is to bring that to 17 per cent by 2030, as part of the growth of an indigenous timber processing and export industry; forests also constitute a useful sink for atmospheric carbon dioxide. Since 2000 the aim has been to plant around 50,000 acres per annum, with around 70 per cent of the afforestation carried out privately. Due to the hesitation of private foresters, and the fall-off in state planting, this target has not been met, exacerbating the impact of the destruction of existing forests by fire.

5

The issue of control burning has sometimes caused divisions within communities: farmers argue that media advertisements advising the public to report any fire they see are having a negative impact, while residents who fear the effects of fire have become distrustful of neighbouring landowners. In an effort to resolve such tensions in the Muckross area of Killarney, where farmland meets suburban housing, local people drew up a joint five-page strategy for dealing with control burning and wildfires. They proposed requiring landowners to contact the fire service before a burn and to stay with the fire during a burn. Local residents were asked to create fire breaks and to take other steps to protect their properties from fires, and bodies such as Coillte and the National Parks and Wildlife Service were asked to create and co-ordinate patrols of areas in danger of burning from mid February to mid May – as was done in the past – and to offer a burning service to organizations and landowners not in a position to do their own. The strategy document also sought an extension of the legal burning period to 15 April.

Experts such as Ciaran Nugent believe this kind of community-wide approach offers the only real solution to the problem of wildfire. Stretched national resources mean policing and prosecutions will have only limited impact, and there are concerns that a top-down, authoritarian approach merely fosters an 'us and them' mentality on the part of farmers. Nugent plans to organize test burns, where landowners will be trained in the practice of burning, as part of his drive to encourage farmers and other stakeholders to take ownership of the issue.

On the day I met him, Nugent drove me just outside Killarney, on the Cork road, to see some of the mountainous sites at risk from fire. He showed me the *fionnán* grass, growing long beside good farmland, which he said would go white and dry in the spring. 'Then it stops being grass and we just look at it as fuel.' He showed me commonage divided between two landowners, with gorse on one side and, on the other, soil that appeared black and burnt, which Nugent said had likely been washed away by some of the four thousand millilitres of rain that fall annually in Kerry. 'He's been burning, burning, burning. The sheer amount of rock on that hill suggests to me that the soil on that land is depleted,' he said. He showed me a house, set into a hilltop, with thick clumps of tall yellow gorse clustered beside and behind it. Then he showed me another hilltop, which he termed his 'nightmare'. The hilltop was shrouded in a wall of gorse, maybe six or seven years old, and it spilled into a large forest plantation. At the front of the wall of gorse sat an electricity transmission system. 'I would suspect at some point that planta-tion is at risk,' he said. 'Maybe you can get a machine in there that can deal with that gorse, but again the size of it … if that goes on fire I don't fancy anyone's chances of actually controlling it.' For a while we sat silently looking at the mountain, imagining the consequences, and then I jumped out of the car to take some photographs. To one side, set inside a neatly trimmed gar-den, but nestling at the foot of the mountain, stood a single white bungalow.

6

When it rains in Donegal, the low dark clouds meet the tops of the hills and mountains and trees. During my first visit to the county, in early June of last year, the rain fell in solid sheets of grey across the rolling landscape, muting its colours to a muddied mix of brown and grey and green. I spent most of that day in the car, avoiding a soaking, but in the moments when the down-pour eased I stepped out onto the hills and bogs and took photographs of vivid green grass growing in clusters out of the blackened soil.

The land had not yet completely lost its wounded look. Along the route from Glenties to Dungloe, I could see places where the fires had jumped the road and come close to houses. After a while, I pulled in to a hillside, where I could see a forest of burnt trees a short walk away. The trees were conifers around twelve feet high. When I touched them, the carbon came off on my hands. They stood in charred bogland, on either side of a mucky, grassy path-way that must have been carved out with a digger, and the smell of the burn hung heavily in the air. The scene was silent, and it was desolate.

On my way back up the hill I stopped and looked out over the land in the distance. I could see only a few houses, but there were acres of fields and many more forests. The fields were still green, but the forests all looked the same. Broad lines of black ran parallel to each other, indicating the way the fires had travelled in straight lines up the forest drains; these lines were interspersed with narrower lines of orange and amber and brown and white, where the leaves and branches of trees not directly in the path of the fires had been burned or singed. Here and there, where the trees had not been affected, were some small patches of green. Before I reached the car, I passed a couple of signs. 'No shooting,' said the first. 'Trespassers will be prosecuted,' said the second.

Later that day, I visited the remains of Ursula Stein's house, near Ballyshannon. A chimney stack was still standing, and the base was intact, but the walls were gone. In what had been the interior of the house, the floor was covered in a thick blend of white and black flakes of chalk and stone, and scattered about it were a bath, a sewing machine, an oven and a hob, twisted from the heat of the fire. There were some jugs and cups and some broken plates. There were pieces of shrivelled glass. At the back, tall conifers that must have huddled against a wall had been burned orange and black. At the front, only the tidy green garden and the neatly sculpted path had escaped. The lawn still looked freshly cut, and some yellow and purple flowers swayed in the breeze.

The rain had stopped, and the sky was pale pink and blue. White and grey clouds drifted slowly across it. I thought of how Ursula Stein might have died in the Donegal fires and of what, if she had lost her life, might then have been said and promised about the problem of wildfire in Ireland.

Remaining calm: A diary for 2011

IAN SANSOM

Saturday 1 January

All that remains of the snowman is the tinsel, two sticks, two lumps of coal, and a carrot.

This year I am going to remain calm. All year.

A friend has recommended to me a book about meditation, *Mindfulness in Plain English*, by Bhante Henepola Gunaratana, who is a Buddhist monk. According to Bhante G – as he is affectionately known, apparently, by his friends – meditation will teach me to become 'like a perfect parent or an ideal teacher'. I will feel love towards others and will achieve 'a profound understanding of life'. This sounds excellent.

I am also reading Mark Vonnegut's *Just Like Someone Without Mental Illness Only More So* (2010), which is a memoir about his madcap father Kurt Vonnegut, and about his own struggle with mental illness. The book does not suggest that writers are perfect parents or ideal teachers who feel love towards others and have a perfect understanding of life. On the contrary. 'Writing is very hard mostly because until you try to write something down, it's easy to fool yourself into believing you understand things. Writing is terrible for vanity and self-delusion.'

'I might have to give up writing in order to achieve enlightenment,' I tell my wife.

'Fine,' she says. 'You do that.'

Tuesday 11 January

John Gross, the great literary critic and editor, is dead. I met him a couple of times, years ago. All I can remember is that he wore very large glasses – like

Muriel Spark's – and he urged me not to pursue the life of a freelance reviewer and writer. Didn't listen; total lack of forethought and self-insight.

'This knowledge of reality in your experience helps you to foster a more calm, peaceful and mature attitude toward your life' (*Mindfulness*).

Saturday 22 January

Andy Coulson has resigned. He is – something like – Director of Communications for David Cameron. And he edited *The News of the World*. How could anyone have thought it was a good idea to have the former editor of *The News of the World* as Director of Communications?

Friday 28 January

On the way to work I look out of the train and see there is no traffic on the dual carriageway. It turns out that a woman who'd tried to jump off the bridge near IKEA earlier in the week has now alas succeeded in hanging herself from the bridge.

In Egypt, Hosni Mubarak says he'll go later this year.

All week I have been running training courses on communication for community and voluntary groups in Belfast – groups from what are still referred to as 'the two communities'. There are not just two communities, obviously: there are never just two of anything. But, some interesting differences emerge. Asked for examples of great communicators, one group – representative of one of the two communities – suggest Noam Chomsky, John Pilger and Robert Fisk. Asked the same question, another group – same kind of group, same kind of people, but representative of the other community – suggest Peter Kay, Jimmy Carr and Chris Moyles.

At one session I am assisted by a stenographer. I have never worked with a stenographer before. She types as I speak, glancing at me continually because I am speaking far too fast. In the morning I peak, apparently, at 325 words per minute, at which point she gives up. Normal speed is 200 words per minute, she says.

'Sorry,' I say. 'I'm nervous.' She is not impressed. Over lunch I ask how she ended up as a stenographer. She tells me a story of such tragic loss that I am left speechless. In the afternoon, I try to slow down. Three hundred words per minute. Still no good.

At another session a man refuses to participate. He simply folds his arms and says 'I'm not doing that.' 'Fair enough,' I say. 'You're like Bartleby.'

I'm maybe not cut out for these training courses.

On the way home I read about the sentencing of two people – one of them a young, public-school-educated woman – for the manslaughter of Ian Baynham, a gay man, back in 2009. They kicked and punched and beat him to death in Trafalgar Square.

Thursday 3 February

The woman in the café has been doing a creative-writing course. She is wearing vivid, extraordinarily bright green eyeshadow and no other make-up whatsoever – she looks as if she's a modette on a scooter on her way to a Caister weekender sometime in the early 1980s.

At work, in a meeting, there is a long, complicated discussion about 'rubric violations'. I don't understand the rubric, or the violations.

Am struggling with the mindfulness thing. Reading Gogol instead, everything I can about Gogol. Have fallen in love with Gogol. Why have I never read Gogol before? He comments that he has an urge to collect 'all this prosaic rubbish of life, all the rags, down to the smallest pin, that swirl around a person every day'.

Friday 4 February

To friends for dinner – an annual invitation. A is back from the oil rigs. He's put on a bit of weight: he says all there is to do is work and eat curry. C is off the Prozac.

Monday 7 February

In the park, waiting to pick up son, get talking to a man sitting on a bench. He has a farm up in the Craigantlet Hills. I ask how's the farming. He says, 'It's coming on to lambing time.' I say I know nothing about lambing. He says, 'And you just keep it that way.' And then he says, 'Can you do me a favour?' And I say yes, if I can, I will. I have never met this man before. We have spoken for maybe two minutes. But I like him. 'Can you tell me what's the best book you've read in the past twenty years?' It is an unexpected question, at 6 p.m. on a Monday, in the dark, in the park. He's read all the classics, he says, Russian, French, English, German, everything, and he's always looking for something new. And the bigger the better. Challenging. He likes a big book for lambing every year, he says, so he's got something to read through the night. Last year he read all of Haruki Murakami. What did he think? Overrated, he says. I suggest Philip Roth. 'Ah,' he says, 'a Roth-head, are you, eh?' He's already read a couple. 'Not as a good as John Dos Passos,' he says.

Thursday 10 February

Someone has used plastic bags woven into a wire fence at Bridge End station to spell out a message, but it has been obliterated by the wind and rain. The only letters that remain are 'A' and 'T'. On the train I am reading *Conversations with Saul Bellow*, ed. Gloria L. Cronin and Ben Siegel (1994). 'I have always put the requirements of what I was writing first – before jobs, before children, before any material or practical interest, and if I discover that anything interferes with what I'm doing, I chuck it. Perhaps this is foolish, but it has always been the case with me.' There's a Yiddish phrase: *nisht vert ken tsibele*.

Mubarak still hasn't gone. The *Today* programme sent James Naughtie over – a sure sign that your despotic regime is about to fall – but to no avail. Naughtie now back in England.

I give a reading in a library. Six people turn up, which is four more than the last time. 'You're the next big thing,' says my wife, later.

Two women sit at the very back of the room. Middle-aged. One of them has a face as if she's had a stroke. The other is puffy-faced, raddled looking. They whisper to each other the whole way through the reading. It would be embarrassing to tell them to be quiet. When I finish the reading the puffy-faced woman puts up her hand and says, 'So, basically what you're saying is that we're not good enough for you, eh?' I don't think I said anything controversial or disdainful – but then I am English. Maybe that was it. The women get up and walk out. Does this happen to Geoffrey Hill?

Wife has been working away from home all week. Eldest son has flu, has been off school. Daughter has vomiting and diarrhoea.

Friday 11 February
Wife returns from London, with baklava.

Saturday 12 February
Mubarak finally goes, as if to spite James Naughtie.

Monday 14 February
School half-term. Take children to London for a couple of days. Go on a 'Duck Tour', in which we drive around the streets and then into the Thames in an amphibious vehicle. I attempt to explain to the children about Thor Heyerdahl and the *Kon-Tiki* expedition, but confuse the Pacific with the Atlantic. The tour guide says of his driver, 'I met Chris at drama school. Things have turned out well for the both of us.'

Wednesday 16 February
Music awards ceremony on TV last night. Woman called Adele sang a song, 'Someone Like You'. Not really my cup of tea, but incredible performance. Heartfelt. Wife and children know all about Adele already. Turns out I may be the only person in western Europe who has never heard of Adele.

Wednesday 23 February

The papers are calling it the Arab Spring – first Tunisia, then Egypt, now Bahrain and Libya all in turmoil. My wife is reading all the papers, every day. I can't keep up. Also, seem to have hearing loss in left ear – upper quadrant of my head seems not to resonate, feels dead. Occasionally I feel like banging this part of my head on a wall to wake it up. 'Don't do that,' advises my wife. 'Go and see a doctor.'

Someone gives me a lift in their BMW. I haven't been in a posh car for years. The BMW has heated seats.

Saturday 26 February

On the train, two men in the seats in front, old-fashioned skinheads, English, smelling of drink, talking loudly and getting louder all he time. They start banging on the window.

'Fucking brilliant! How thick are these fucking windows!'

'A quarter of a fucking inch thick, mate!'

They bang on the windows with their fists and shout 'Dildo!' and 'Cunt!' as loudly as possible. I am considering how exactly I might approach them to ask them to be quiet when an elderly man gets in before me and tells them to keep it down.

'Yeah, right, fucking mint, mate!' yells one of the men at the old man.

'Fucking train!' says the other, slightly quieter. 'Fucking quieten down!'

'Stena Plus on the Stranraer Ferry is fucking mint, mate!' says the first man, even more quietly. '£10 and free lattes and nibbles. You can easily eat at least £20 worth of nibbles and you're first on, first off, no fucking messing about! It's the fucking way forward, I tell you. Stena fucking Plus.'

Thursday 10 March

My mother rings at 8.20 p.m. She says, 'Just to let you know that George has … gone.' George is my father's older brother. He's been in a home.

Alzheimer's, cancer. Worked all his life for Newham Council, in London, as a gardener. His wife died many years ago, and his daughter, Denise, of a brain tumour. 'So that's the end of that story,' says my mum.

Wednesday 16 March

News from Japan getting worse and worse. Massive earthquake a couple of days ago; tsunami; nuclear reactors have exploded. Today, several newspaper headlines contain the word 'Apocalypse'.

A group of young women get on the train at Ely. Birthday celebration. They have five bottles of champagne, a pack of vodka mixer drinks, a bottle of actual vodka, and three bottles of wine. It's 10 a.m. The woman whose birthday it is keeps shouting, 'I'm twenty-one and I'm riding tonight!' The conversation concerns men, shoes, handbags. 'When I'm pissed, don't let me break the toilet again and get shit all over myself like last time.'

In the UK unemployment has hit 2.5 million.

Friday 25 March

Fly to England with eldest son for uncle's funeral. We are flying Flexible Economy, which means we can use the Business Lounge and are entitled to breakfast on the plane. We are both looking forward to it. Son is tempted to eat dozens of the free biscuits in the Business Lounge. I persuade him to wait for slap-up breakfast.

On the plane, the fine-featured lady stewardess, with expensively honey-blonded hair and carmine-red nail varnish, apologizes, there's been a catering problem. There are no breakfasts.

We only just make it to the crematorium, due to my miscalculating how long it might take to get from Heathrow, west London, to Upminster, east. We arrive at Upminster station at 11.23. Funeral is at the crematorium at 11.40, a twenty-minute drive away. My father drives like a maniac. We make it with one minute to spare.

My father gives the memorial address. To prevent myself from crying I stare fixedly at the cobwebs high up on the ceiling in the chapel – grey, swaying, like ectoplasm, the stuff of death itself. Death has got another of us and is coming for the rest, just like in Bruegel's *The Triumph of Death*.

Outside, a large floral tribute in the shape of a Smirnoff vodka bottle, with the words 'NANA' picked out in red.

There is a kind of wake in a social club, which is advertising for a 'Ladie's Nite.' Son claims he's seen the place on *My Big Fat Gypsy Wedding*.

At the security gate at Stansted a man is dressed as a giant penis. Neither he nor his friends seem to be particularly enjoying the joke. He attempts to go through the scanner with the penis suit on. The security guy tells him to remove it.

Finally, late, driving home, a man in a bright red shirt is running in the road, against the flow of traffic, as if he were fleeing from disaster and we are hurtling towards it.

Saturday 26 March

Read obituary of Nikolai Andrianov, a gymnast who held fifteen Olympic medals: 'At his peak as a gymnast, Adrianov's powerful musculature allowed him to perform with impeccable technical and artistic finesse, but in recent years he had developed a rare degenerative neurological disorder called multiple system atrophy. He was unable to move his arms or his legs, and he could not speak.'

Unseasonably warm weather. Short-sleeve weather. Quarter of a million people protest in London against government cuts. Some demonstrators occupy Fortnum and Mason.

'Plenty of caviar to keep them going, then!' I say to my wife.

'That's not actually funny, you know,' she says. 'I'm going to stop bringing the *Daily Mail* home from work. You're starting to sound like Richard Littlejohn.'

Monday 28 March

Over dinner, filling in the UK census. We ask the children which box they wish to tick, identity-wise. Eldest son says British. Younger son says Northern Irish. Daughter says Irish. 'And you?' says my wife.

'I very much see myself as a citizen of the world,' I say.

'I'll put you down as English, then.'

Wednesday 30 March

On the bus, two women are talking.

'I've bought myself a car.'

'A car?'

'Yes. Though I've had it a month and not used it once.'

'You should try a couple of lessons.'

'I'm not sure ...'

'You should. It's too late for me now, and I suppose I've still got Bobby to run me around. What colour is it?'

'Red.'

'Like lipstick?'

'Yes, but I wouldn't know which.'

Friday 1 April

Election posters everywhere. Up by Finaghy Methodist church in Belfast we notice the poster for Alex Maskey, of Sinn Féin. Younger son says, 'Why isn't he smiling? Everyone else is smiling.' He's right. Alex Maskey seems to be the only candidate who isn't smiling in his election poster. He looks like he's about to punch you in the face.

Sunday 3 April

Catholic police constable Ronan Kerr has been killed in Omagh by a car bomb.

Monday 4 April

A colleague gives me two pens as gifts: an Esterbrook dollar pen, mottled sil-ver, like a herring, and a little Japanese Sailor pen with a fine nib. I like the Esterbrook pen so much I start writing my novel again. Simple as that.

On TV, a programme about the consequences of obesity, *Dead Fat*. A funeral director explains that he has to use a winch and a crane to get people into their coffins. Ten o'clock news: they are firing on people in Yemen, there is a no-fly zone over Libya, and some kind of massacres in Ivory Coast.

Am moving into a smaller office at work – was only squatting in the big-ger office, which is really someone else's. Moving books, I flick through John Anthony Cuddon's *Dictionary of Literary Terms and Literary Theory* (4th edn, 1998), and by chance turn to the page in which he describes a genre of novels concerned with what he calls the 'superfluous man'.

Thursday 7 April

Man on the radio talking about his diet book. He says he practises a form of aversion therapy: foods that he shouldn't eat he simply imagines as bad. He does not explain what these imaginings might be. Just for fun I imagine: bread excreted by a giant baker; rice as maggots scooped from the guts of Chairman Mao; pasta the boiled heart fat of a dead obese Italian; and pota-toes simply as rocks.

Make spaghetti bolognese. Can't face it.

Friday 8 April

Man on a submarine shoots his fellow crew members. Surprised it doesn't happen more often.

A man in a meeting says that he is 'ashamed' and 'embarrassed' at having to explain something to me again. Shaming and embarrassing on all counts.

Tuesday 19 April

We go to a Mr Crawford's house, on a new estate off the ring road. In his garage he has twenty second-hand pianos: it's a big garage.

When we bought our house the piano came with it – none of the children would have learned had it not been left behind. It's an Ajello, made by Craig & Sons of Belfast, ancient, out of tune, full of woodworm – it'll be sad to see it go.

In Mr Crawford's garage I like the Steinhoven, which has a rich choco-latey tone, and the Zender, which is a church-hall kind of piano, with a lot of oomph and cut-through. But I don't play the piano. Younger son likes the Yamaha: it's shiny. We say to Mr Crawford, if we were to buy one, when could you deliver? He looks at his watch and says, after 5.30 this evening? Sure enough, he arrives with a friend, takes away the old Ajello and slots the new one into place. Tuneful, shiny. Don't miss the Ajello at all.

Wednesday 20 April

Daughter is going to a friend's 'Coketail' party. Which is a cocktail party, only with Coke. She wants to have her hair styled. My wife is working away, and I am not capable of styling hair, so I take daughter to a proper ladies' hairdresser. Haven't been to a ladies' hairdressers since my mother occasion-ally took me a 'unisex salon' with her in Essex in the 1970s. It's amazing. Like a film-set Manhattan loft apartment. I am offered coffee and a range of maga-zines, while daughter's hair is styled. I could get into this. It's like being in a gentleman's club. Except for the hair. And the ladies.

Friday 22 April

The weather has been so warm – so good – for so long that the government has issued a smog warning in the south of England. Even here it's nice. Older son has taken to going to 'beach parties', where huge groups of teenagers gather on the beaches along the coast between here and Belfast to drink and snog. I am concerned about the beach parties. 'It won't last,' says my wife. 'The weather'll turn.'

Sunday 24 April, Easter

So warm we decide to have a barbecue, but the barbecue disintegrated and rusted a long time ago, so we simply dig a pit in the garden, build a fire and balance an old grill pan on top, filled with sausages. Then we watch *Britain's Got Talent*, in which an irate, terrible stand-up comedian tells the audience to 'beep' off, and a 91-year-old man performs a song from *Fiddler on the Roof* with his 21-year-old granddaughter, and a woman attempts to sing with her dog.

I go to bed with an atlas and attempt to learn the capital cities of all countries beginning with A. Capital of Armenia?

Wednesday 27 April

Another year, another Newtownards ballet festival. A *Wizard of Oz* routine danced by one little girl, who plays Dorothy, the tornado, the Scarecrow, the Tin Man, the Lion, the Munchkins, the Wicked Witch, Toto, *and* the flying monkeys. In its way, a tour de force.

The Real IRA say they are going to kill police officers and that the Queen is a war criminal.

Friends invite us round. They have had their garden redesigned for a TV garden-makeover programme. 'It's incredible,' I say. 'Like something you'd see on the telly.' 'Obviously,' says daughter.

Andrew Marr, TV and radio journalist, has been revealed as the person who took out a super-injunction to prevent the press reporting on his extramarital affair. He says in an interview that he feels 'uncertain' about the ethics of it – meaning not the affair but the super-injunction.

Reading E.M. Forster's *Commonplace Book*, ed. Philip Garden (1985): 'my three nibblers – kindness, lust and fun. My enemies they are not, there is not enemy but cruelty. But they waste me and diminish me – especially kindness

... Tolerance, easiness, laughter, even sympathy have their leaky aspects, and while exercising them – as I do – something essential drains away.'

Also reading Norman Lebrecht's book about Mahler, in which he quotes Mahler writing about his time as artistic director of the Vienna Court Opera: 'My job absorbs me completely and seizes me body and soul, I am swamped as only a theatre director can be ... All my senses and emotions are turned outward. I am becoming more and more a stranger to myself ... Remember me as one usually remembers the dead.'

Thursday 28 April

Go with older son to Caz, the Turkish barber. Caz is having bench seats put in the shop, to replace the chairs. 'What colour do you think for the uphol-stery, Mr Sansom? Burgundy?' I agree that burgundy would be a very fine colour indeed. 'And Chesterfield style? What do you think?' He makes me a cup of Turkish coffee and then cuts son's hair.

Old man comes in. I've seen him in the shop before. He has learning diffi-culties. Caz is very nice to him. Makes him laugh. The man has clumps of hair growing around his neck, and ear hair, and big tufts of hair on his bald-ing head. 'What's wrong with you?' says Caz. 'You want to scare the ladies away looking like King Kong?'

Another man comes in, sits down next to me, sees that I am reading a book about Mahler. He says, 'You like Mahler?' I say yes. We talk about Mahler. He likes Mahler. Then he says, 'Wait here, I have something for you,' and he goes away and comes back with a big sheaf of papers about Messianic Jews. 'This is for you,' he says, 'please read it.'

'How was the barber's?' says my wife.

'Oh, you know, the usual.'

Friday 29 April

Royal Wedding. 'Can we have a fry?' asks older son. 'In celebration?'

Dutch friend comes round for coffee. She is a big fan of the British royals.

Monday 2 May

Bank Holiday. Woke at 7, to the news that Osama bin Laden has been killed by US Special Forces in a compound in Pakistan. And the Mountains of Mourne are burning, with vandals setting fire to the gorse.

In the evening we are invited to a barbecue. Other families there, our age. Doctors, lawyers, professional people. People we have never met before. They have polite teenage children who look like the models in a Benetton catalogue. During the course of the evening our friends mention to their nice friends that I am a writer. It's almost worth never leaving the house so that people don't mention this to other people, because there is only one inevitable question, with one inevitable answer.

'Will we have read anything of yours?'

'No.'

'Oh.'

End of conversation.

Wife reprimands me when we get home.

'It's better to get it over and done with,' I say.

'It's a conversation,' she says. 'Not a police interview.'

Tuesday 3 May

Older son cooks his signature dish – chicken curry – for dinner. Delicious. Younger son wants to go out and meet his friends. We insist he stay and eat the dinner. Older son eats extra slowly. Younger son so frustrated that he punches his brother with all his strength on the side of his head, knocking him off his chair. Brawl ensues. All-round confiscation of mobile phones, computer-time, visiting privileges.

Tuesday 10 May

Fly to Milan for Italian book tour.

(This sounds so good that in my notebook I write it twice.)

Fly to Milan for Italian book tour.

Go for a walk in the park opposite the hotel, late afternoon. There is that dry, delicious afternoon heat, people playing with their Italian-looking children, little bars and cafés everywhere, and an old-fashioned carousel, and a couple becoming intimate, and a beautiful young woman riding a beautiful decrepit old bike, with a beautiful little dog in the basket, and I sit in a bar drinking beer, and there is a courtyard with marble floors and statuary and it is exquisitely quiet, and the sun is reflected off the walls of the mustard-coloured buildings with the olive-green shutters and it is hard to believe (a) that this place exists at all and (b) that I am here.

Meet my Italian publishers: Elena, Stefano, Elisabeth. We walk through the streets of Milan, to the Duomo and a restaurant which has a terrace overlooking the Duomo, and I am eating risotto with saffron and we are talking about books and life as the sun goes down and I think, 'Any moment now I am going to wake up and this is all going to be a dream.'

Instead, I go to the bathroom and find that my fountain pen exploded on the plane on the way over: my shirt is stained dark blue; it looks as though I have been shot in the stomach and have been bleeding ink.

Wednesday 11 May

Wake up, breakfast, wander down towards La Scala – which is smaller than you think. Interviews with journalists and photographs, 10–5, and then a taxi to the station for train to Turin and a few days at the Book Fair, where there are more interviews, a photoshoot for *GQ* magazine, and I am staying in the old Fiat car factory, which has been converted into a luxury hotel, and my translator is a woman who speaks five languages – 'FLUENTLY,' she says, 'plus some others less so' – and we eat out every night and I meet Italian writers and critics and publishers and when my wife, not having heard from me for a couple of days, texts 'ALL OK?', I reply, simply, 'Fine.'

Friday 13 May

Return from Milan to discover that Henry Cooper is dead, Sinn Féin have gained another seat in the local elections, the DUP have gained two, and the weather finally has broken.

Saturday 14 May

Go to horrible out-of-town retail unit, to buy daughter a hamster. We have been promising to buy her a hamster since her birthday earlier this year. We go for a dwarf Russian. I suggest we call him Gogol. Daughter calls him Snowy.

In Germany, John Demjanjuk, 91-year-old guard at Sobibor death camp, is sentenced to five years in prison. My father and I disagree about this. My father thinks leave him be.

Wednesday 18 May

The Queen is in Ireland.

Thursday 19 May

One of the judges of the Man Booker International Prize resigns because she disagrees with the award being made to Philip Roth – apparently he 'goes on and on and on about the same subject in every book. It's as though he's sitting on your face and you can't breathe.' Curious conceit, but … accurate.

Tuesday 31 May

Have taken to the Irish habit of attending the funerals of friends' and colleagues' family members. Funeral of a friend's father, who left school at fourteen, worked in the shipyard all his life, never said much about himself, attended church every week. Friend says, 'We'll not see his like again.'

I ask my wife to read, at my funeral, the closing lines about Dorothea, from *Middlemarch*: 'But the effect of her being on those around her was incal-

·culably diffusive: for the growing good of the world is partly dependent on unhistoric acts; and that things are not so ill with you and me as they might have been, is half owing to the number who lived faithfully a hidden life, and rest in unvisited tombs.'

My wife says, 'I don't think so.'

'Why not?'

'Self-pitying perhaps? And vainglorious, simultaneously?'

It's good to have a wife for such purposes.

Friday 3 June

Mindfulness still not working. Must be doing something wrong. My wife insists instead I read a book, *Yes, Your Teen Is Crazy!* The main message seems to be: be nice; stay calm.

Daughter announces that she has had 'the talk' in school.

'How was it?'

'Fine. I knew it all already.'

'Really?'

'Yes. Mum told me ages ago.'

Like a sitcom dad I somehow missed this.

Saturday 11 June

Unexpectedly, we have no children. They're all out. Wife suggests we go for a picnic on Tyrella beach. We used to go there when the children were young. We buy some picnic-type supplies at the garage in nearby Clogh. There's a sign saying 'Deli': turns out it's a chilli-chicken, build-your-own-bap type of thing. Stick with fruit and crackers.

Beach deserted, except for rubbish blowing everywhere. Freezing cold. We sit down. Within ten minutes a group of fifty children arrive on an outing, sit down next to us and start playing rounders. We move further down the beach. A couple arrive and sit down five metres from us. We retreat to the car, eat our fruit and crackers and drive home.

Saturday 25 June

County Down Fleadh, 10 a.m. The Ards Under-12 Comhaltas Grúpa Cheoil are practising for their classes outside Warrenpoint Town Hall, daughter playing harp. Harp string snaps – middle C. This is not an optional string. I do not have a spare middle-C harp string with me. Go to Diarmuid McQuinn's music shop. Mr McQuinn has no harp strings in stock, but he does know a woman in town who plays the harp. He kindly gives me her number. So I am ringing a complete stranger, a woman, in Warrenpoint, on a Saturday morning, to ask if she might be able to assist with me with a harp crisis. The woman could not be more understanding. But she does not have a spare middle-C string.

'You could borrow a harp,' a friend suggests. It's worth a try. I go up to another harpist and ask if we might be able to borrow her harp. Alas, again, no. I ask another harpist. No. And another. Ditto. 'Actually, I didn't think that would work,' says my friend. 'People can be very funny about their harps. It's like asking to borrow their child.'

Nothing to be done but go ahead with middle-C string missing. Fortunately, the plucky Ards Under-12 Comhaltas Grúpa Cheoil surge through their set – 'Eleanor Plunkett', 'Kilnomona's Barn Dance', 'A Fig for a Kiss' – and are placed first! A magnificent triumph over adversity! On to the Ulster Fleadh!

Saturday 2 July

Son leaves for scout camp in Canada at 5 a.m. One mother says to me, of her own son, 'I don't know what I'll do without him.' I come back home and go back to bed.

Watch a programme on TV in which Rufus Wainwright is attempting to write a song with Guy Chambers, who apparently writes songs with Robbie

Williams. Mr Chambers seems nice – cuddly. Mr Wainwright seems …
fraught.

Friday 8 July

Following son's activities in Canada on a blog set up by the scout leader.

The News of the World is going to close.

Saturday 9 July

Friends' wedding at a place called the Wapping Project, in London, not far
from where my grandparents used to live. Wapping has gone up in the world
since I was young. Guests at the wedding include Seamus Heaney, Karl Miller,
Daniel Craig, Miranda Richardson.

'What are we doing here?' I ask my wife.

'We're invited,' she says.

Sunday 10 July

Mother rings at 6 a.m. My dad was rushed to hospital at 2 a.m. Burst appendix.

Tuesday 12 July

Outside Liverpool Street Station a young man has a sign around his neck:
'Need Someone to Talk To? Confidential Chat Over a Coffee or Lunch.' And
then, in smaller writing underneath, 'You Buy the Coffee.'

Another man is wearing a tiger suit and has a sign that says 'I Will Dance
For Anyone For £1.' No one asks him to dance.

Universities are going to charge tuition fees up to £9,000.

Wednesday 20 July

Father out of hospital.

At the parliamentary select committee to answer questions about phone-
hacking at *The News of the World*, a protester throws a shaving-foam pie at

Rupert Murdoch. Murdoch's Chinese wife fights back.

We go to the cinema to see *Kung Fu Panda 2*, in which the eponymous panda is advised to find his inner peace. He should try *Mindfulness*.

Saturday 23 July

Ulster Fleadh in Dungiven, St Patrick's College. Traffic jam stretching almost all the way back to the Glenshane Pass. Former students of St Patrick's include the folk singer Cara Dillon and Eoghan Quigg, a teenager with a memorable hairstyle who was a finalist some years ago on *The X Factor*. Children impressed.

Alas, the Ards Comhaltas Grúpa Cheoil do not qualify for the All-Ireland Fleadh in Cavan. We buy All-Ireland Fleadh T-shirts instead, almost as good.

Sunday 24 July

In Norway, crazed gunman went to a political rally being held on an island and shot dozens and dozens of people. But didn't then shoot himself, which suggests he is not as crazy as most crazed gunmen, merely evil.

Tuesday 2 August

Older son cuts his head open while out playing in a wood. At A & E, he asks the doctor sticking his scalp together, 'Is it just superglue?' 'Yes,' says the doctor.

While waiting, a woman comes in, carrying a little freezer bag. I can't see what it is – assume it's her lunch. Sausage roll? Sushi? She sits waiting for a couple of hours, hand held high, wrapped in a huge white fluffy towel. Eventually, a doctor comes rushing out to her. She says, 'Shall I bring my thumb with me?'

Thursday 11 August

Go to NHS travel clinic for various jabs in advance of a trip to Brazil. Didn't know the NHS ran travel clinics. The nurse says, 'If you are planning to have sex with the locals, I would advise using a condom. And don't go the dentist. Or get bitten by a dog.'

Saturday 13 August

The rioting in London seems finally to have stopped. People were breaking into shops and setting fire to buildings. Three men killed in Birmingham. Man beaten almost to death in Ealing, half a mile from where we used to live. Newspapers are in paroxysms: one of the looters is at university; another is eleven; another works in a primary school; there are endless interviews with a woman who jumped out of a window of a burning building, and with an old black woman who confronted the rioters and who is – inevitably – a 'YouTube sensation'.

Robert Robinson has died. I wonder what Robert Robinson and the panel on the old Saturday-night *Stop the Week* would have said about the riots? Milton Shulman. Benny Green. Something witty, something wise.

Monday 15 August

Trip to Carréducker, bespoke shoemakers in Cockpit Yard, London, WC1N. Am making a programme about shoes for Radio 3. For the purposes of the programme I am fitted for a pair of bespoke shoes. Feet measured, I then get to choose my fantasy shoe. I go for a Derby boot with brogue-style ornamentation and cleated rubber soles, made of cordovan leather. They will take six months to make, explains the lovely shoemaker, Mr Ducker. And how much will they cost? He mentions a four-figure sum. But this includes shoehorns, he says. And repairs. I ask who buys these sorts of shoes, at this sort of price? 'All sorts,' says Mr Ducker. 'But mostly oligarchs.'

Tuesday 23 August

Fly to Brazil for Brazilian book tour – more improbable even than Italy. No matter how many times I write it down it won't seem real.

The young woman sitting opposite sobs uncontrollably for most of the twelve-hour flight.

'Good you're here on a Wednesday,' says my jovial bear-like translator, Marcelo, as I hobble through arrivals, exhausted and hungry. 'Why?' 'Feijoda!' he says, slapping me on the back, laughing and lighting up a cigarette. Driving around São Paolo at breakneck speed we discuss the meaning of life, American imperialism, the work of the great Brazilian writer Clarice Lispector, the London riots, the Clash, modern jazz, Judaism, Islam, world poverty, and the use of torture by military dictatorships. It's one of those sorts of journeys. Favelas stretch for miles, with Sky dishes on every roof. A Michael Jackson impersonator moonwalks across a six-lane junction, begging for money as he goes.

Feijoda, it turns out, is the Brazilian national dish, brought over by the Portuguese settlers and eaten by tradition on Wednesdays. It is made with black beans, salted pork, bacon, pork ribs and smoked sausage, and it comes with various traditional side dishes, including the Brazilian equivalent of pork scratchings. Basically, it's pork. It is absolutely delicious.

One night, we are invited to a concert where a band of old guys play traditional samba and people get up out of their seats and dance. It's warm, everyone is relaxed, and we are in a beautiful old theatre: it's like being in a movie. I realize that I am in terrible danger in falling in love with the first woman I meet, changing my name to Rafael or Bruno, becoming a beach bum, and never returning to Northern Ireland. It is for this very reason that my wife is travelling with me.

Another night, we are at a sushi restaurant where there is karaoke downstairs, a wall-to-wall live televised MMA cage-fighting tournament upstairs, Pink Floyd's *Dark Side of the Moon* being piped loudly on speakers throughout, and Brazil's leading cross-dressing cartoonist holding forth on the state of the world, while outside the preacher in the open-storefront Assemblies of God church is yelling 'Hallelujah!' again and again and again until the early hours.

I like it here. A lot.

Friday 2 September

What's to report? Back to old routine. School. Work. Protesters staged a demonstration during the Israel Philharmonic's concert at the BBC Proms. Concert taken off air.

Thursday 27 October

'A former Rotary Club president and his ailing wife used a Rolls-Royce to fill their garage with fumes in a double suicide pact, an inquest was told. Bill Warburton, 67, of Botley, west Oxford, was found dead at the wheel of the car while his wife Mary, who had suffered balance problems since 2005, sat close by in her wheelchair. Verdict: suicide.' *Daily Telegraph.*

Friday 4 November

Wedding of friends' daughter, officiated by one of the Singing Priests, Father Eugene O'Hagan. I had not previously heard of the Singing Priests, who are … singing priests. They have a record deal with Sony. Older women at the wedding all wearing purple. Like a meeting at the Vatican.

Saturday 24 December

Read in the paper of the death of Caroline Walsh, literary editor of the *Irish Times.* Stunned. Like a lot of people, I absolutely adored her. She was brisk, rude, funny. Seemed to be able to take everything seriously, without taking anything too seriously.

Don't know what to say.

Christmas, again.

Notes on contributors

RACHEL ANDREWS is a freelance journalist based in Cork. Her piece on the Maze prison site appeared in *Dublin Review* 39.

ANTHONY CALESHU's most recent book is *Of Whales*, a collection of poems.

DONALD MAHONEY is a freelance journalist of no fixed abode. His piece on the rise and fall of a Burren pizzeria appeared in *Dublin Review* 45.

PHILIP Ó CEALLAIGH's most recent collection of short stories is *The Pleasant Light of Day*.

ED O'LOUGHLIN's most recent novel is *Toploader*.

TIM ROBINSON's most recent book is *Connemara: A Little Gaelic Kingdom*.

IAN SANSOM's most recent novel is *The Bad Book Affair*.